Bubble Troubles

Mattie & Mark Miller · Double Trouble

WANDA E. BRUNSTETTER

BARBOUR
PUBLISHING

Cover illustration: Colleen Madden/MB Artists

Published by Barbour Publishing, Inc., P.O. Box 719, Uhrichsville, Ohio 44683, www.barbourbooks.com

Our mission is to publish and distribute inspirational products offering exceptional value and biblical encouragement to the masses.

 Member of the
Evangelical Christian
Publishers Association

Printed in the United States of America.
Dickinson Press Inc. Grand Rapids, MI; April 2013; D10003846

DEDICATION

To Sara Beth,
a very special Amish schoolteacher.

GLOSSARY

absatz—stop
ach—oh
amberell—umbrella
appeditlich—delicious
baremlich—terrible
bauchweh—stomachache
bruder—brother
bu—boy
daed—dad
danki—thanks
deich—pond
dumm—dumb
frosch—frog
gfarlich—dangerous
grummbier—potatoes
Guder mariye. —Good morning.
gut—good
gwilde—quilt
hund—dog
hungerich—hungry
jah—yes
katze—cats
kichlin—cookies
kinner—children

kumme—come
lecherich—ridiculous
maedel—girl
mamm—mom
melke—milk
Mir hen bang gat. —We were afraid.
naerfich—nervous
rege—rain
schmaert—smart
schnee—snow
schtiffel—boots
umgerennt—upset
vergeksagdert—terrified
Zaahweh is schlechdi kumpani. —A toothache is a bad companion.

Contents

CHAPTER 1

Worrywart

"What are you doin' with that?" nine-year-old Mark Miller asked when his twin sister, Mattie, came out of the house with her umbrella.

"I'm taking my *amberell* to school in case we get *rege*," Mattie replied. "Come to think of it, maybe I should go back in the house and get my rubber *schtiffel*, too."

"Just hold on a minute, Mattie!" Mark pointed to the blue sky above. "There's not a single cloud this morning, so I don't think it's gonna rain. . .which means you don't need an umbrella or rubber boots. Besides that, I can always smell rain when it's comin', and I sure don't smell it right now." He motioned to the porch. "You oughta just leave the amberell on the porch so we can get moving. We don't wanna be late for school, ya know."

Mattie frowned. "Oh Mark, quit your fussing. We're not gonna be late. We still have plenty of time to get there."

"But don't forget—we're walkin' to school today, Mattie, so it'll take us longer to get there." Their bicycle built for two had a flat tire, and Dad hadn't found the time to fix it yet, so the twins had no choice but to walk. "We won't get to school before the bell rings if you keep foolin' around," Mark said.

"I'm not fooling around." Mattie slipped the umbrella into her backpack. "And I'm takin' this to school just in case it does rain."

"Whatever." Mark didn't know where his sister had gotten the silly notion that it was going to rain today. Anyone could look at the sky and see there wasn't even a hint of rain. It was clear and blue and one of those mornings you could see for miles. "You worry too much, Mattie," Mark said as they hurried out of their yard. There were times, like now, when he didn't think he'd ever understand his sister, even though she was his twin.

There were many things Mark and Mattie didn't agree on or see the same way. Mark liked to tease and fool around, and Mattie was more serious about things. But then their differences made them special, and as Grandpa Miller often said, "The twins are unique."

"I do *not* worry too much," Mattie insisted. As she started walking faster, a wisp of red hair came loose from the stiff black cap she wore on her head. Sometimes Mattie wore a dark head scarf, but not on the days she went to school. She mostly wore it around the house or when she had chores to do.

"You've been worrying a lot lately," he insisted. "Last week you were worried about the fog. Said you didn't think we could find our way to school 'cause the mist was so thick. But we made it just fine and got there on time. Remember, Mattie?"

"*Jah*, of course I do." She slowed some and turned to look at him. "Why do you always have to remind me whenever I'm wrong about something?"

"I'm not tryin' to rub it in or anything," he said. "I was just tryin' to make a point."

"What kind of point?" she asked.

"The point that you sometimes make an issue of things when you oughta just learn to relax."

Mattie didn't say anything. Just blinked her blue eyes a couple of times and started walking again, even faster this time.

"So what's making ya so jumpy today?"

"Nothing. I just remember the last time it rained on the way home from school, we got soaking wet," she said. "I won't let that happen again."

"It's a nice fall day, with no clouds in the sky, and you're worried about rain?" Mark asked, walking real fast to try and keep up with her. "You know what you are, Mattie?"

"What?"

"You're a worrywart!" He chuckled. "Jah, you're nothin' but a silly little worrywart!"

"No I'm not."

"Jah you are."

"I like to be prepared," she said with a huff.

"So do I, and I'm prepared for sunshine today." Mark lifted one hand toward the sky while he held on to his lunch pail with the other.

Mattie didn't say a word.

As Mattie sat at her school desk that morning, she kept glancing out the window, watching the sky. There were a few white, puffy clouds, but not a hint of rain, just like her brother had said.

Maybe Mark was right, she decided. *Maybe it won't rain today after all. But I'm glad I brought my amberell, just in case.* Mattie wanted to be prepared. It was better than ending up soaking wet. Like Grandma Miller often said, *"The weather can be quite changeable at times."*

"Mattie, did you hear what I said?" Their teacher, Anna Ruth Stutzman, touched Mattie's shoulder.

Mattie jerked her head. "Uh, no. Guess I didn't."

"I asked if you did your homework over the weekend."

Mattie gave a quick nod, thankful she'd gotten her assignment done.

Anna Ruth smiled and said, "That's good. Now, would you please hand it to me, like the other scholars have done?"

Mattie's cheeks warmed. She'd been so busy staring out the window watching the clouds that she hadn't even heard the teacher ask the class to turn in their homework. She opened her backpack, pulled out the folder with her math assignment inside, and handed it to her teacher.

"Thank you, Mattie." Anna Ruth gave Mattie's arm a gentle pat, and then she returned to her teacher's desk at the front of the room.

Mattie liked her teacher. Anna Ruth had light brown hair, hazel-colored eyes, and a pretty face with a pleasant smile. Although she didn't tolerate any fooling around in class, Anna Ruth was always kind and patient.

Mattie's friend Stella Schrock, who sat in the seat behind her, tapped Mattie on the shoulder. Stella had dark brown hair, matching eyes, and a creamy complexion, with not even one freckle on her face. Not like Mattie, who had several freckles.

Mattie turned her head toward Stella. "What do ya want?"

"Did you bring your jump rope with you today?" Stella whispered.

Mattie shook her head. "The last time I brought the jump rope, it got caught in my bicycle chain, remember?"

"No talking, girls." Anna Ruth put one finger to her lips. "You're supposed to be copying your spelling words." She pointed to the blackboard, where she'd written all the words. "You'll need to learn these for the upcoming test."

Mattie frowned. Not only had she been caught talking in class, but she also had a list of spelling words to copy, and some of them looked kind of hard.

Before Mattie started writing, she glanced over at her brother, who sat across from her. He stopped copying the spelling words long enough to frown at her, and then he put his head down and went right back to work.

Mattie looked away and tried to focus on each of the words. She could only imagine what Mark would say when they went outside for recess. Most likely she'd get a lecture from him, since he always did well with his studies and rarely talked out loud in class. Mark was especially good at spelling, so he probably thought the words Anna Ruth had given them were easy. *I'm sure he'll pass the spelling test,* Mattie thought. *But not me. I'll probably fail.*

The test would be given at the end of the week, and Mattie was worried. Thankfully, she had a few days to prepare, and maybe if she studied really hard, she would get at least some of the words right. Mattie would have to work twice as hard as Mark. But if that's what it took for her to pass the test, then she was prepared to do it.

"I told ya it wasn't gonna rain today," Mark said as he and Mattie walked home from school that afternoon, following their brothers, Calvin and Russell, who were some distance ahead on their bikes. "See, you were worried for nothing." He looked at Mattie and noticed her frown. "What's wrong? Are ya *umgerennt* because you brought your amberell to school for nothing?"

She shook her head so hard that the ties on her bonnet swished around her face.

"Then what's wrong? Why are you frowning?" he asked, bending down to pick up a small flat rock. It would go nicely with his collection of other unusual rocks.

"I was thinking about those spelling words the teacher gave us today," Mattie said. "Some of them are really hard."

"No they're not. I think most of 'em are pretty easy," Mark said. "In fact, I can spell every one of those words without even studying, and I can write 'em in a sentence, too."

"Really?"

"Jah. Here I go. . . Scarecrow. S-c-a-r-e-c-r-o-w. Mom put a scarecrow in the garden to keep the birds away. Toothpaste. T-o-o-t-h-p-a-s-t-e. Some people in our family forget to squeeze the toothpaste from the bottom." Mark waited to see what Mattie would say, since she was one person in the family who often forgot to squeeze the bottom of the toothpaste to make sure there was plenty at the top. But Mattie said nothing— just kept plodding along.

"Popcorn. P-o-p-c-o-r-n. One of my favorite winter

snacks is popcorn." Mark continued with his words and sentences. "Volleyball. V-o-l-l—"

"Okay, that's enough." Mattie stopped walking and tapped Mark on the shoulder. "You know you're *schmaert*, and I know you're smart, so you don't have to rub it in."

"I'm not trying to rub it in," Mark said. "I just wanted you to see how easy those spelling words are."

"They might be easy for you, but they're not for me. I always have trouble with spelling." Mattie sighed. "I'm worried I might fail the test."

"There you go again. . .worrying about something that may never happen." Mark grunted. "Just study those words, Mattie. I'm sure you'll do fine."

"I shouldn't have said anything," Mattie mumbled. "I knew you wouldn't understand."

"I do understand. I'm good at some things, like spelling, and you're good at other things, like playing ball. Why don't you try writing each word down several times until you're used to spelling out the word? You could be better at spelling if you'd study harder."

"And you could be better at baseball if you'd practice running and throwing the ball more often," she said. "We need to play catch sometime."

Mark knew Mattie was right, but he didn't like playing baseball. He had trouble catching the ball, and he couldn't run as fast as the other kids, either. He was the one who always got teased by some of the boys in their class because he couldn't play as well as they did. What made it worse was that his twin sister could play ball better than he could. Mattie was a fast runner and could hit and catch the ball better than most of the boys. Because she was so good at baseball, and Mark wasn't, he didn't play unless their teacher said he had to. But that was a lot different than studying for a test. It was important to get good grades in school.

"By the way," Mattie said, "do you know how we got that scratch on the back fender of our bike? I noticed it the other day when our tire went flat."

Mark wondered why Mattie would even care about something like that. "Probably happened during one of the times we fell, when we were learning how to ride the bicycle built for two," he said.

"We'd better ask Dad if he has any paint. We don't want it to start rusting where the scratch is," Mattie said.

"There you go, worrying again," Mark complained. "I'm sure that scratch has been there awhile. Why are you fretting about it now?"

"Never mind, Mark. I'm sorry I even mentioned the scratch." Mattie shifted her backpack, and Mark figured it was heavier than usual today. *Too many books, and her amberell,* he thought. *She really should have left it at home.*

The twins walked the rest of the way home in silence. Mark was eager to get there so he could play with his two cats—Lucky and Boots. Of course, he wouldn't be able to do that until he'd done all his chores.

"Where's Twinkles?" Mattie asked Mom after they got home. "I didn't see her outside anywhere, and I called for her several times."

A wisp of Mom's pale auburn hair came loose from the stiff white cap she wore on her head as she shrugged her shoulders. "I don't know. I haven't seen your dog since you fed her this morning. Did you put Twinkles in the kennel before you left for school?"

"No, I forgot." Mattie's forehead wrinkled. "Maybe she's in the barn. Did you, by any chance, look for her in there?"

"No, Mattie," Mom said, shaking her head. "I've been busy all day, washing clothes and taking care of your little brother and sister. Besides, I assumed Twinkles was in her kennel, where she usually is during the day."

"I need to hurry and change my clothes; then I'm goin' out to look for her," Mattie said, eager to find her dog.

"I'm sure Twinkles didn't go far, and you can look for her after you've done your homework," Mom reminded. "You, too," she added, looking at Mark.

"I don't have any homework," he said. "I got it done during recess today."

Mattie groaned. "Can't I do my homework after supper?"

"No," said Mom. "You need to do it now, because Grandma and Grandpa Miller will be joining us for supper, and I'm sure you'll want to spend some time with them after we eat."

"That's true," Mark put in. "It's always fun to listen when Grandpa tells stories about when he was a *bu*."

Mom chuckled. "That's right, and I think your grandma likes to tell stories about when she was a *maedel*, too."

"I wonder, when I grow up, if I'll be tellin' stories about when I was a boy," Mark said, taking a bite of the molasses cookie Mom had just handed him. "Yum. . . this sure is *gut*."

"*Danki*," said Mom. "I'm glad you like it." She gave one to Mattie as well. "Now tell me what *you* think, Mattie. Are the *kichlin* as good as usual?"

Mattie took a bite and bobbed her head. "Jah, Mom. The cookies are very good. They're moist and chewy, just the way I like 'em."

Mark lifted the remainder of his cookie to his nose and took a sniff. "They smell really good, too. I love the aroma of ginger in them." He looked over at Mattie and grinned. "In case you didn't know it, *aroma* means *smell*."

Mattie grunted. "I figured as much."

"Would you two like some *meilke* to go with your cookies?" Mom asked. "When Calvin and Russell got home, I gave them some cookies and milk, but they took theirs out to the barn."

"Jah, please," the twins said at the same time. They often did that when someone asked them a question. Mattie figured it was because they were twins and sometimes thought the same thing. Of course, even though they looked similar, with red hair and a few freckles, they were really not that much alike. Mattie liked dogs; Mark liked cats. Mark was a tease; Mattie wasn't. Mark collected marbles and rocks; Mattie liked to decorate things with flowers. In many ways, they were as different as night and day.

While Mom poured the milk, Mark and Mattie took seats at the table.

"How was school today?" Mom asked. "Did you learn a lot?"

Mark nodded eagerly. "After I finished my homework during recess, I looked for some new words in the dictionary." He gave Mom a wide grin. "I found one I really like, too."

"What is it?" Mom questioned.

"*Obstinate*," Mark replied, looking over at Mattie. "It means *stubborn*."

Mattie rolled her eyes. "You should have been outside playin' baseball during recess, not looking up big words."

"I agree with your sister," Mom said. "You ought to go outside and play at recess like the other children do, not stay indoors. You really need the fresh air and exercise."

"I go outside sometimes and push the little kids on the swings." Mark looked at Mattie and wrinkled his nose. "And for your information, I like big words. They're fun to say, and I like finding out what they mean in the dictionary." Mark thrust out his chin. "And ya know I don't like playin' ball."

Mattie made no reply. She finished her cookies and milk, put her dishes in the sink, and took today's homework out of her backpack. While she worked on the spelling words, Mark went upstairs to change his clothes.

When he came back down, he stopped to see how Mattie was doing. "It might help if ya break the spelling words down." He pointed to her paper. "See. . .tooth and *paste* become *toothpaste*. And *pop* and *corn* become *popcorn*. If you take it a little at a time and write each word down several times, it might be easier for you," he said with a grin.

"Danki, Mark." Mattie couldn't believe how nice her brother was being. Sometimes he liked to tease her, but other times, like now, he was kind and helpful.

"You're welcome." Mark went over to Mom, who stood at the kitchen sink, peeling potatoes. "I'm going outside to do my chores now. When I'm done, I'll be in the barn playing with my *katze*," he said, before hurrying out the back door.

Mattie wished she could go outside and look for Twinkles right away, but she knew she'd be in trouble if she didn't get her homework done, so she continued to write out the words the way Mark had suggested.

"I'm going to see if Ada and Perry are up from their naps now," Mom said. "As soon as you finish your homework, you can go outside and look for your *hund*."

Mattie smiled. "Okay, Mom."

After Mattie wrote the spelling words down, she decided to get her math questions done. She knew she should write each spelling word more than once, but she had until Friday to take the test. So when the math questions were finished, she put her homework away and went upstairs to change her clothes.

Mattie also made a mental note to remember to ask Dad about paint for their bike fender so it wouldn't get rusty. She'd study the words more later on. Right now, there were too many other things to think about, like where did Twinkles get to, and would she ever come home?

As soon as she'd changed into her everyday dress, Mattie tromped down the stairs and hurried out the back door.

"Here, Twinkles!" she called from the back porch, clapping her hands as loudly as she could. "*Kumme*— come here, girl!" Mattie looked toward the field where the hay had been harvested, knowing Twinkles often liked to play in there. She hoped to see the dog come bounding toward her. Unfortunately, there was no sign of Twinkles, not even a bark.

Mattie checked Twinkles's dog dish and noticed that

only a little of the food had been eaten. "That's strange," she said, shaking her head. Normally Twinkles ate all of her food while Mattie was at school. She must not have been very hungry today. Either that or she hadn't been here most of the day. *Sure wish I'd put Twinkles in her kennel before we left for school this morning,* Mattie thought with regret.

Mattie searched all over the yard, but she couldn't find Twinkles anywhere. Then she raced into the barn, where she found Mark sitting on a bale of straw, holding both of his cats in his lap.

"Lucky and Boots missed me today," he said, smiling at Mattie. "As soon as I sat down, they leaped right into my lap and started purring." Lucky was the mother cat, and Boots was her baby. Lucky was fluffy and gray. Boots was black with four white paws.

"That's nice," Mattie said. "Have you seen Twinkles out here in the barn?"

Mark shook his head. "If she was here, she'd probably be chasin' my katze. Then I wouldn't get to pet them at all, because they'd be hissing, howling, and runnin' all over the place, trying to get away from your mutt."

"Twinkles is not a mutt." Mattie placed both hands on her hips. "She's a cute little terrier, and I'm sad that she's missing!"

Mark flapped his hand like he was swatting at a pesky fly. "Don't be so melodramatic, Mattie. I'm sure she's not missing. Probably just doesn't wanna be found."

Mattie squinted her eyes. "What does *melodramatic* mean?"

"It means you're exaggerating."

"I'm what?"

"You're makin' too much out of Twinkles being gone," Mark said. "She's probably running around somewhere, havin' a good ol' time. Maybe she's out in the field chasin' some of those wild rabbits we've seen around our place."

"But I've called and called for her, and I didn't see any sign of her in the field. Oh Mark, what if she doesn't come home soon? It'll be dark in a few hours, and she might freeze to death out there on her own." Mattie shivered, just thinking about it.

Mark groaned. "You're being melodramatic again, Mattie. It is kind of chilly at night, but it's not so cold that Twinkles would freeze to death. And I don't think she's scared of the dark."

Just then, Mattie spotted Twinkles's dog collar lying next to some wooden boxes in one corner of the barn. When she picked it up, a lump formed in her throat. "Maybe Twinkles has been dognapped!"

"What are you talkin' about?" Mark tipped his head to one side and squinted at Mattie.

"You've heard of people who've been kidnapped, right?"

Mark gave a quick nod.

"Well, I'm worried that someone may have stolen my dog, and they took off her collar so no one could identify her."

"That's just plain *lecherich*," Mark said. "Who'd want to take your *dumm* little hund?"

Mattie shook her head. "It's not ridiculous, and Twinkles isn't a dumb little dog. I'm sure lots of people would want her. Stella said once that she wished she could have a dog like Twinkles. My hund's not only sweet, but she's a very schmaert dog." Mattie sniffed and swiped at the tears running down her cheeks. "I—I don't know what I'll do if she doesn't come home. If anything happens to Twinkles, it will be my fault for letting her run loose today. Oh, I wish I had put her in the kennel before we left for school!"

CHAPTER 2

Muddy and Wet

Mattie had a hard time going to school the next day. Twinkles was still missing, and Mattie was worried she might never see her cute little pet again. She wished she could stay home from school and search for Twinkles or at least be there if her dog returned home. But Mom had ushered Mark and Mattie, along with their brothers, Russell and Calvin, out the door as soon as breakfast was over.

Now, as they trudged along toward the schoolhouse, Mattie kept an eye out for Twinkles. "Here, Twinkles!" she called. "Where are you, girl?" There was no sign of the dog—not even a bark or a yip.

Normally, on the way to and from school, Mattie enjoyed looking at all the pretty wildflowers in the fields or listening to the birds that flew overhead. Except for the crows, the blue jays were about the only birds squawking from the trees today. Right now, even though it was late in the season, there were still some goldenrod and asters and also the purple ironweed flowers blooming. One thing about wildflowers—there was always something blooming from early spring until late fall. Mattie could only admire the goldenrod, though, since their little brother, Perry, was allergic to them. Mom really liked it whenever Mattie picked flowers for the table, but unfortunately, today Mattie wasn't in the mood to pick any. All she could think about was her poor little dog out there someplace, but who knew where? Mattie had been so upset last night that she'd slept with Twinkles's dog collar under her pillow. "Here, Twinkles! Here, Twinkles!" she called once more.

"You're gonna lose your voice if you keep hollerin' like that," Mark said. "And my ears will be ringing soon if you don't cut it out."

"But I've got to find my hund." Mattie sniffed and glanced all around, hoping and praying Twinkles would come bounding up to her, swishing her little tail.

"She'll come home when she's ready."

"Not if someone took her."

"I don't think anyone took her, Mattie. Just try not to worry so much."

Mattie frowned. That was easy for Mark to say. It wasn't his pet who'd gone missing. She wished Dad had fixed their flat tire last night. She could have spent more time looking for Twinkles this morning if they'd been able to ride their bike, because it would have gotten them to school a lot quicker.

When they arrived at the schoolhouse, Mattie told Mark she was going to ask some of the girls if they'd seen Twinkles anywhere.

"That's a good idea," Mark said. "I'll ask the boys. Maybe some of 'em will have information about your hund."

Mattie raced over to a group of girls who were playing on the swings. "My dog's missing," she said, trying to catch her breath. "Have any of you seen her lately?"

"Not me," Becky Hostetler said with a shake of her head.

Mattie's friend Stella brought her swing to a stop. "I haven't seen Twinkles, either."

Mattie looked at the other two girls—Anna and Karen Troyer, who were sisters. They had also stopped swinging. "What about you? Have you seen my dog?"

"No," they both said.

"How long has Twinkles been missing?" Stella questioned.

"She disappeared sometime yesterday, while I was at school." Mattie blinked several times, trying to hold back her tears. Talking about Twinkles and how much she missed her made Mattie feel sad. She was so worried that her stomach had begun to ache.

Stella got off the swing and gave Mattie a hug, while the other girls went back to swinging. "I'm sorry, Mattie. I really like Twinkles, and I hope you find her rcal soon. I'd come over after school to help you look for her, but Mom's taking me shopping for new shoes."

"That's okay, Stella. I hope we find her soon, too. I miss Twinkles so much," Mattie said, grateful for the support of her best friend.

"Did you ask all the boys if they'd seen any sign of Twinkles?" Mattie asked Mark as they walked home from school that afternoon.

"I did, and no one's seen your hund," he replied, wishing he didn't have to give her that news. "Don't worry, Mattie. If Twinkles isn't there when we get home, I'll help ya look for her."

"Danki, Mark. That means a lot to me."

Even though earlier Mark had told Mattie not to worry, he felt bad that Twinkles was missing. After talking to his friends and hearing that no one had seen the dog, Mark was nearly as disappointed as he knew Mattie must be. Truth was, he'd be worried, too, if one of his cats had disappeared. Even though Twinkles often got on his nerves, he was still concerned about the dog. It wasn't like Twinkles to be gone this long—especially without food, because that playful dog sure liked to eat.

"How'd you do on the math test we took today?" Mark asked, hoping to change the subject, as they neared their home. He knew the more they talked about Mattie's missing dog, the worse she'd probably feel.

"Not very well." Mattie sighed. "All I could think about was poor Twinkles, out there somewhere on her own."

"Try to relax, Mattie. We're almost home, and if she isn't there, we can start looking for her."

"Probably not till our homework and chores are done," Mattie said. "You know Mom always makes us do those things first."

"Well, I don't have any homework, 'cause I got mine done during recess again." Mark gave Mattie's arm a pat. "As soon as I finish my chores, I'll start lookin' for Twinkles. When you're done, you can join me."

"Okay." Mattie looked grateful when she smiled at him, and Mark felt good about offering to help her find Twinkles. Deep down, he wished he could find the dog by himself. He'd love to see the look on Mattie's face if that were to happen.

When the twins went inside the house, Mom greeted them at the door with a cheery smile.

"Did Twinkles come home today?" Mattie asked with a hopeful expression.

Mom shook her head. "I'm sorry, but I haven't seen any sign of your dog at all."

Mattie's chin trembled. "Mark and I want to go looking for her. Is it all right if we go now?"

"Of course you can search for her, but you need to get your chores and homework done first," Mom reminded the twins. "If your little brother and sister wake up from their naps soon, maybe we can all go looking for Twinkles."

"I did my homework at school again today," Mark said. "So all I have to do is my chores."

Mom nodded. "That's fine. You can search for Twinkles as soon as you're finished."

"If we don't find Twinkles today, can we put some LOST DOG signs around Walnut Creek?" Mattie asked.

"Sure, we can do that as soon as we've had our supper this evening," Mom said.

"Where are Calvin and Russell?" Mark asked. "I didn't see their bikes outside. Thought maybe they could help us search for Mattie's dog."

"They went to the store to get a few things I need for supper," Mom replied. "They shouldn't be gone too long."

Mark gave a nod, and then he bounded up the stairs to his room and hurriedly changed his clothes. When that was done, he went outside to muck out the barn while Mattie worked on her homework at the kitchen table. When he was finished with his chores, he headed for the house to see if Mattie was done with her homework so they could begin looking for Twinkles. He was halfway there when it started to rain. By the time his feet hit the porch, it was pouring.

"You two had better stay inside for now," Mom said when Mark came in the house and stood on the throw rug because his shoes were wet. "If you go outside to look for Twinkles right now, you'll be soaking wet."

"But Mom," Mattie said, her eyes filling with tears,

"if Twinkles is out there in the rain, she'll get wet, too."

"I'm sure she'll take care of herself and find a place to get out of the weather." Mom gave Mattie's shoulder a squeeze. "Animals have an inner sense about things. Now please stop worrying and get your homework done."

That evening during supper, Mattie could hardly eat anything on her plate. Never mind that Mom had fixed chicken and dumplings, which were always so good. Mattie had no appetite for food at all. Her stomach felt like it was twisted into one big knot. It was still raining outside, and all she could think about was her poor little dog out there somewhere by herself, getting wet. Twinkles was probably cold and hungry. She might even be scared.

"Where's Twinkles?" Mattie's three-year-old sister, Ada, suddenly asked. Ada had red hair like Mattie's, and she got excited easily—especially when Mark made silly faces at her.

Mattie looked at Ada, unable to answer her question. How could she explain that her dog had run away? Ada liked Twinkles and was bound to cry if she found out the dog was missing. In fact, every time Ada saw Twinkles, she would get all excited and wave her hands, squealing with delight.

Mark came to Mattie's rescue and tickled Ada under her chin. She giggled and wiggled and waved her hands.

"Twinkles is on an adventure and will come home when she gets tired," Mark said when Mom told him to stop tickling Ada so she could eat the rest of her supper.

That seemed to pacify Ada, for she quickly finished eating the chicken and dumplings on her plate. "All gone!" Ada said, lifting her arms and grinning at Mom.

"I'm done, too," Mattie's five-year-old brother, Perry, announced as he rubbed his belly. Perry had thick blond hair like Dad's.

"Okay, you two," Dad said, placing his hands on Perry and Ada's heads. "Wipe your faces, and we'll go into the living room and play for a bit, until it's time to have our dessert."

Mattie forced herself to finish eating her chicken and dumplings. If it stopped raining and she was allowed to search for her dog after the dishes were done, she would need plenty of energy to help accomplish that task. Mattie knew that unless Twinkles came home, there would be no dessert for her tonight. The apple pie Mom had baked today didn't sound appealing right now— not even the way Mattie liked to eat it, with a scoop of vanilla ice cream on top.

When supper was over, Mattie helped Mom clear away the dishes. She dragged her feet slowly from the table to the sink, with the worry she felt about Twinkles making her feel tired.

"Come on, Mattie. I can see that you're really sad," Mom said as she washed the dishes and stacked them for drying. "You need to remain positive and ask God to watch over your hund."

Mattie hoped Mom was right, and although it was difficult, she told herself that everything would turn out fine and that God would protect her cute little dog.

Mattie had just put the last dirty dish in the sink and was going to start drying the ones Mom had already washed when she heard a scratching sound at the back door. *I'd better see what that noise is,* she thought. *Maybe, just maybe, it's Twinkles.*

Mattie dried her hands on a towel and opened the back door while holding her breath.

Yip! Yip! Yip! Twinkles, all muddy and wet, darted into the house, wagging her short little tail.

"*Ach*, Twinkles, it is you!" Mattie shouted. "I'm so happy you're home!"

"*Absatz*—stop!" Mom hollered, quickly closing the kitchen door so the dog couldn't run through the rest of the house. "Catch her, Mattie, and then you'd better fill the tub and give that hund a bath. I won't allow her to run though the house with muddy, wet feet."

Mattie scooped Twinkles into her arms, not even caring that her dress was getting wet and dirty. "I don't know where you've been all this time," she said, giving Twinkles a hug, "but from now on I'm gonna put you in the kennel whenever I'm gone. I want you to be safe and stay in the yard. You had me so worried, and I don't want you runnin' off ever again!" Mattie held Twinkles tightly, never wanting to let her go. She had missed her little four-legged friend, and even though she didn't know where Twinkles had been, she was ever so thankful the dog had come home.

Mom smiled. "As soon as you've given Twinkles a bath, you can help me make some popcorn. And don't forget about the apple pie I made earlier today. We'll have some of that, as well."

"Can we have some of Dad's apple cider, too?" Mattie asked. Now that Twinkles was home, she was in the mood for dessert. In fact, her appetite had suddenly reappeared.

"Of course, and I'll get out some vanilla ice cream to go with the pie," said Mom. "Now hurry along."

Mattie laughed as Ada starting waving her hands, and Perry jumped up and down when they came into the kitchen and heard Mom mention ice cream and pie. Feeling light on her feet, and humming softly as she held Twinkles close, Mattie headed for the bathroom to fill the tub. Now her stomach growled with hunger, when only a few minutes ago she could hardly eat a thing on her plate. All of a sudden, she was starving for apple pie and ice cream. It felt good to be relieved of all that worry.

Just outside the bathroom door, Mattie stopped and whispered a prayer: "Thank You, dear Jesus, for bringing Twinkles safely home."

CHAPTER 3

A Good Week

"You're awfully quiet back there," Mark said as he and Mattie rode their bike to school on Friday morning. "Are ya daydreaming again?"

"No, I'm not," Mattie replied. "I'm thinking about the spelling test we're supposed to take today." She was glad Dad had fixed their tire last night and they could now pedal quickly to school.

"You shouldn't be *thinkin'* about it," Mark said. "You should be practicing the words."

"I'm practicing them in my head."

"Humph!" Mark grunted. "You oughta say the words out loud. That's the best way to remember how to spell 'em."

"You really think so?"

" 'Course I do. I'll tell you what, Mattie," Mark said. "I'll say a word, spell it out loud, and then make a sentence using that word. After that, you can say another word and do the same."

"Okay."

"Popcorn. P-o-p-c-o-r-n. I love to eat popcorn."
Mark glanced over his shoulder. "All right, Mattie, it's
your turn to say a word now."

"Tearful. T-e-a-r-f-u-l-l. I was tearful when Twinkles
was lost."

"I don't think your hund was lost, Mattie. She just
didn't come home till she was good and ready. Oh, and
you spelled the word *tearful* wrong."

"Did not."

"Did so. You put two *l*'s at the end, and there's only
one. It's t-e-a-r-f-u-l, not t-e-a-r-f-u-l-l."

"Oh, guess I forgot. Let me try another one," Mattie
said.

"Nope. It's my turn now."

"Okay, go ahead." Mattie figured whatever word
Mark chose from the list, he'd know how to spell it. She
wished spelling came as easy for her as it did him, but
then, most of the things they learned in school seemed
easy for Mark.

"The word I choose next is *flabbergasted*," Mark
announced.

Mattie let go of the handlebar with one hand and
poked her brother's arm. "That word isn't even on our
list. You made it up, didn't you?"

"Nope, but you're right, it's not on the list. I'm gonna
add it to the list so I can get extra credit," Mark said.

She frowned. "Don't see why you have to do that.
I'm sure you'll get all the spelling words right, so you

shouldn't need any extra credit."

Mark shrugged his shoulders. "I don't care. I like big words, and I'm gonna add it to my list."

"What does *flabbergasted* mean?" Mattie questioned.

"It means shocked or amazed."

"I see. Well, don't expect me to add any words to my list. It'll be a miracle if I can spell the words that are on the list now. I'm really worried I might fail the test. I probably didn't study as much as I should have, 'cause I was so worried about Twinkles."

"There you go again, Mattie. You're worried about somethin' that might not happen. Just practice the words some more and do your best when we take the test." Mark slapped his knee and laughed. "I just rhymed my words: *Do your best when we take the test.*"

"I will do my best," Mattie said, although she already felt somewhat defeated. "I'll practice the words in my head all the way to school."

When it came time to take the spelling test that afternoon, Mattie's stomach knotted up again. Her hands grew so shaky she almost dropped her pencil. When the teacher said each of the words, Mattie concentrated and tried to sound them out in her head. It was a good thing she'd practiced the words on the way to school; otherwise she might not remember how to spell any of them right now.

"And now the final word on the list is *worry*," Anna Ruth told the class.

That one should be easy for me, Mattie thought, chewing on her pencil eraser. She wrote the word down on her paper then made a sentence using the word. "Mark says I worry too much."

"All right now, class, pass your papers to the front of the room."

Mattie did as the teacher asked. She'd done her best on the test. Now she had to wait until the end of the day to see how well she'd done.

During recess that afternoon, Mark's best friend, John Schrock, tried to get Mark to join the game of baseball some of the other children were playing. John was Mattie's friend Stella's cousin, but he didn't look anything like her. Stella had brown hair and brown eyes. John's hair was blond, and his eyes were blue.

"Huh-uh." Mark shook his head. "You know I'm not good at playin' ball."

"Aw, come on," John coaxed. "You don't play that bad."

"Jah, I do." Mark frowned. "I get tired of the other kids makin' fun of me because I don't run fast enough." Even though he'd been watching the baseball game, Mark kept his distance. He wanted to make sure no one asked him to join in. Mark didn't like to come up with excuses all the time, but it was the only way to avoid being teased if he played the game.

"You should just ignore 'em," John said. "Then they'll get tired of making fun of you."

"Maybe so, but I'd rather not play ball." Mark moved across the schoolyard and leaned against the fence, kicking at a rock before propping his foot on the bottom rail.

John followed. "How do ya think you did on the spelling test?" he questioned.

Mark smiled widely. "Think I did fine. The words were easy."

"Not for me." John shook his head. "Bet I flunked that test."

Mark thumped his friend's back a couple of times. "Now don't start worrying like Mattie does. You probably did better than you think."

"I hope so." John dragged the toe of his boot through the dirt. "So what are you doin' after school? Can ya come home with me and play awhile?"

Mark removed his straw hat and shook his head. "Not without asking Mom first."

John pointed to Mark and snickered.

"What's so funny?" Mark asked.

"You oughta see your red hair right now. It's standin' straight up in the air." John laughed out loud.

Mark reached up and smoothed the top of his hair; then he plopped his hat back on his head.

"Are ya sure you can't come over to my place today?" John asked. "You can call your mother when ya get to my house and see if it's okay."

"That's not a good idea. Mom might not go out to the phone shack to check for messages, so she wouldn't know where I was. Besides," Mark added, "Mattie and I came to school on our bike today 'cause Dad got the flat tire fixed. If I rode over to your house, she'd have to walk home by herself."

"It wouldn't hurt her to do that, ya know. It's not raining today."

"That's true, but it is kinda chilly. I'll bet it won't be long before we have some *schnee*."

John's eyebrows shot straight up. "Ya really think we'll get some snow soon?"

Mark gave a nod. "Could be anytime now that winter is near."

"I can hardly wait for some schnee to start falling," John said. "It's fun to build a snowman, go sledding, or ice-skate on one of the ponds around here."

"I like all those things, too," Mark agreed. "Say, since tomorrow's Saturday, maybe I can come over to your house then. 'Course, I'll have to ask Mom and Dad first, because they might want me to do somethin' else."

"I'll be home all day, so if your folks say it's okay, just come on over." John moved away from the fence. "Think I'll go play ball for a while before recess ends. Are you sure you don't wanna join us?"

"No thanks." Mark watched his friend as he walked toward the game that was now in full swing, with laughter and cheers from those who were playing, as well as from the kids standing on the sidelines watching. He hoped his folks would say he could go over to John's house tomorrow.

"Mom, guess what?" Mattie shouted as she raced into the house after she and Mark arrived home from school that day.

"What is it?" Mom asked, stepping out of the kitchen to greet the twins in the utility room, where they were hanging up their jackets.

Mattie grinned, handing her mother a piece of paper. "I passed the spelling test and only missed two words!" She glanced over at Mark as he showed Mom his. " 'Course, he didn't miss any of the spelling words."

Mom looked at the twins' test scores and gave them each a hug. "I'm glad you both did so well. It sounds like you had a good day."

Mark and Mattie nodded.

"See, you were worried for nothing." Mom gave Mattie's shoulder a gentle tap. "You just need to do your best and train yourself not to worry. As your Grandpa Troyer used to tell me when I was a little girl, 'There are two days in the week you should never worry about— yesterday and tomorrow.' "

"That's right," Mark put in. "Worry gets ya nowhere. Oh, and I think Mattie did well on the test 'cause she practiced the words like I told her to do."

Mom smiled. "I have some apples and cheese slices ready for you in the kitchen. You can have either a glass of milk or some cold apple cider, to go with your snack."

"That sounds good. I'll have some apple cider, please." Mattie smacked her lips. "I'm *hungerich!*"

"I'm hungry, too, but I'll have milk instead of cider," Mark said. "But before we eat our snack, I wanna ask Mom a question."

"What's that?" Mom asked.

"John invited me over to his house tomorrow to play. If it's all right with you and Dad, I'd like to go."

Mom shook her head. "Tomorrow is Grandma Troyer's birthday. Did you forget?"

Mark slapped the center of his forehead. "Oh, that's right. I wouldn't wanna miss that for anything. Guess I'll have to call John and leave a message on his folks' answering machine so he knows I won't be coming over tomorrow."

"I'm excited about going to Grandma and Grandpa's," Mattie said. "I like it when we hire a driver and go all the way to Burton." It was always good to spend time with their grandparents, and with it being Grandma's birthday, Mattie knew the day would be even better. She was sure they'd have lots of fun and that it would be a good day for everyone.

"Do you think Grandma Troyer will make some of her delicious corn fritters while we're there?" Mark asked.

"I don't think we should expect her to do that this time, since it's her birthday we're celebrating." Mom looked at Mattie. "Would you like to help me bake a cake this evening to surprise Grandma with for our dessert tomorrow?"

Mattie smiled and bobbed her head. "That sounds like fun."

"We'll do it after supper," Mom said. "Oh, and I spoke to your grandpa earlier today, and tomorrow evening he's planning to make a bonfire like he usually does when we go there to visit."

"Oh boy! I hope we can roast marshmallows!" Mark exclaimed. "Maybe Grandma will make us some hot chocolate, too."

Mom smiled. "I'm sure she will."

Mattie couldn't wait to see Grandma and Grandpa Troyer, since they didn't get to visit them as much as they did their other grandparents who lived nearby. She was also eager to see if Grandma would like the birthday present she'd made for her. Mattie had saved some of the wildflowers she'd picked a few weeks ago and hung them to dry out. She'd glued them to a piece of cardboard, spelling out the words "I love you" with different pieces of flowers. Mattie even had enough flower parts left over to make a design around the three words. After that, she'd taken an old picture frame she'd bought for a quarter at the flea market a few weeks ago and framed her finished creation. It had turned out quite nice, and she hoped Grandma would think so, too.

What a good week this had turned out to be. First she'd done well on her spelling test, and now she had tomorrow to look forward to. *Guess Mom was right about me being worried for nothing,* Mattie thought.

Feeling like she had springs on her shoes, Mattie skipped into the kitchen, singing, "To Grandma and Grandpa's we will go. . . . To Grandma and Grandpa's we will go. . . . I am so excited. . . . Oh!"

Then Mark joined in, and they both sang at the top of their lungs, "To Grandma and Grandpa's we will go! We're so excited. . . . Oh!"

Grandma Troyer's Birthday

"What are we stoppin' for?" Mark asked when their driver, Tim Norton, slowed his van.

"Looks like there's an accident up ahead," Tim called over his shoulder. "Probably a fender bender. It might have happened because of the rain."

Mark craned his neck. Sure enough, there were two cars with smashed-in fenders, and a police car had pulled up beside them.

"Looks like traffic is tied up a bit," Tim said. "Accidents happen sometimes when the roads are wet."

"And even when they're not," Dad added. "Sometimes drivers follow too close, or else they go too fast."

"You're right about that," Tim agreed. "Whenever I'm behind the wheel of my van, I try to be careful how I drive. I also make sure to watch out for other vehicles. It's important to keep a safe distance from the cars in front of you, in case you have to stop quickly."

Mattie shivered while nibbling nervously on her lip.

"We still have a ways to go before we get to Grandma and Grandpa Troyer's. What if we get in an accident? Maybe it's not safe for us to be on the road today." Mattie tried not to, but she couldn't help looking as the policeman waved them slowly past the accident site. Tim was right—both cars had banged-up fenders. Then she noticed two little girls standing in the wet grass with a lady holding an umbrella over their heads. Mattie assumed it was their mother, trying to comfort the girls, since they looked like they might be crying, although they didn't appear to be hurt. She couldn't be sure about the people in the other car, though, because she wasn't able to see them.

"Now don't start fretting," Mom said, turning to look at Mattie. "Just say a prayer and give your worries to God."

Mattie closed her eyes and bowed her head. *Dear Jesus, please be with us, and take us safely to Grandma and Grandpa Troyer's house. And help those people who were in the accident.*

When the twins and their family arrived at Grandpa and Grandma Troyer's, everyone climbed out of the van and headed for the house.

"See, Mattie," Mark said as they stepped onto the porch, "we got here safely, so you were worried for nothing."

Mattie didn't say anything, just dashed into the house.

Mark tromped in behind her. He didn't understand why Mattie had begun to worry about so many things lately. *My twin sister,* he thought to himself. *Seems like she's always frettin' about somethin'.*

Once they had entered the house, Grandpa and Grandma greeted each of them with a hug. The last time they'd seen their grandparents was when they came to Walnut Creek for Mark and Mattie's ninth birthday, but that had been at the end of summer.

"Ach!" said Grandma, touching Mattie's head. "I believe you've grown a few inches since we saw you last."

Grandpa nodded in agreement.

Grandma and Grandpa both had gray hair, but their blue eyes twinkled as they smiled at everyone. Mark didn't think either of them looked old. Maybe that was because they liked to do fun things and didn't act old.

Mark's joy over being there diminished a bit as he thought about Grandma's comment concerning Mattie's growth spurt. Mark hadn't grown at all in the last few months. It didn't seem right that Mattie was taller than him. They were twins, and he thought they should be the same height.

"Don't worry about it, son," Dad said, as though reading Mark's mind. "I'm sure you'll do some growing soon, too."

Mark wasn't so sure, but he tried not to think about it. He was excited to be there and wanted to have fun. Grandpa usually played a game of checkers with Mark, and he looked forward to that.

Everyone sat around the living room for a while; then Mark and Mattie went outside with their sister and brothers to play on the swings in their grandparents' backyard. Mark and Mattie's older brother, Ike, who was sixteen and had auburn hair like Mom's, stayed inside with the grown-ups. Before Mark had gone out the door, he'd noticed that Ike had been fiddling with his straw hat and looked kind of bored. Mark wondered if his brother would rather be with his girlfriend, Catherine, today, or maybe he wanted to do something else.

I'm glad I'm not old enough to start courting a girl, Mark thought as he returned to the porch. He'd been eager to play a few minutes ago, but now he didn't feel like doing much at all. *Sometimes I wish I could stay a kid forever, but then if I did, I'd never grow up to be tall like Dad.*

Mark plunked down on the steps and rested his chin in his hands.

"What's wrong?" Mattie asked, tromping up the steps and taking a seat beside him.

"Nothin'," he mumbled.

"Jah, there is. You wouldn't be sittin' here by yourself with a glum expression if something wasn't wrong."

"I'm worried," he admitted.

"About what?"

"I'm afraid I might always be short, and then the kids at school will make fun of me." Mark groaned. "It's bad enough that some of the boys call me Flame Brain and Brainiac 'cause I've got red hair and do good in school. I don't need 'em callin' me Shorty now, too. "

Mattie placed her hand on Mark's arm. "You heard what Dad said before. I'll bet you'll have a growth spurt real soon. You might even end up taller than me." Her forehead wrinkled. "Maybe there's something wrong with me 'cause I've grown so tall."

Mark shook his head. "I don't think so, Mattie."

"Well, try not to worry about it." Mattie grabbed Mark's hand. "Come on. . . Let's take turns pushing Perry and Ada on the swing."

"I don't feel like it. I just wanna sit here by myself," Mark mumbled, noticing some oddly shaped rocks in Grandma's flower bed. Normally he would have picked some of them up and taken them home to add to his collection, but he wasn't in the mood for that today. He didn't want to run, swing, or play tricks on anyone, either. He just wanted to sit there and think.

Mattie shrugged. "Suit yourself. If you wanna be an old sour puss, that's up to you, but I'm gonna have lots of fun today!" She jumped up and raced across the yard to the swings.

Mark continued to sit there feeling sorry for himself. A few minutes later, Calvin joined him on the porch. "Look, Mark," he said, pointing to one corner of the backyard. "Grandpa has the branches stacked for the bonfire we'll be having later on."

Mark glanced at the place where his eleven-year-old brother had pointed and gave a brief nod. "Jah, I can see that."

Calvin grinned and pushed a hunk of blond hair away from his eyes. "It'll be fun to roast marshmallows later on, don't ya think?"

"I suppose."

"You sure look unhappy right now." Calvin bumped Mark's arm. "I thought you were excited about comin' to visit Grandpa and Grandma Troyer today."

"I was, but after Grandma said how much Mattie had grown, it made me worry that I might always be short."

"I'm sure you won't be," Calvin said with a shake of his head. "I was short like you once, ya know, and just look at how tall I am now." He stood to his full height and smiled from ear to ear. "Just give yourself some time, and someday you'll be just as tall as me."

Mark hoped his brother was right. "Maybe I'll be *ginormous*," he said, relaxing a bit.

Calvin's eyebrows shot up. "Gi-*what*?"

"Ginormous. It means really big."

Calvin chuckled. "You never can tell about that."

Maybe if I eat more, I'll grow quicker, Mark thought, giving his right ear a tug. *Jah, that's just what I'll do. I'll start eatin' more food.*

"Would someone please pass the *grummbiere*?" Mark asked during supper that evening.

Mom's eyebrows furrowed. "You want more potatoes? But you've already had two helpings so far, not to mention the three pieces of chicken you ate."

"I'm hungerich," he said, reaching for another roll and slathering it with some of Grandma's sweet-tasting apple butter.

"My little brother's a growing boy." Ike chuckled and poked Mark's already full stomach. "Least he will be if he keeps eating like that."

Russell, who was thirteen, bobbed his blond head.

"It's not good to overeat," Grandma said. "You might end up with a *bauchweh*."

"That's true," Dad agreed. "You don't want a stomachache, do you, Mark?"

Mark shook his head. "But if I eat more, I might grow quicker."

"You'll grow fat but not tall." Ike snickered.

"Your big brother is right," Mom said. "If you eat too much on a regular basis, you might become overweight, but it won't help you grow any taller."

"What will help me then?" Mark questioned.

"Time is what you need." Grandpa Troyer spoke up, giving his full gray beard a quick tug. "You'll grow taller when the time is right. I thought we'd had this discussion already."

"Mark's worried that the kids at school might start calling him Shorty," Mattie announced before Mark could respond.

"If they do, just ignore them," Mom said. "I don't think they will, though. Not unless you bring attention to the fact that Mattie's taller than you."

"Some of the other kids our age aren't real tall, either." Mattie smiled at Mark. "You're taller than my friend Stella Schrock."

Mark didn't say anything as he finished eating his roll and reached for another piece of meat. By the time supper was over, he was so full he could hardly get up from his chair. Maybe he'd been wrong to stuff himself like that. If he was going to eat more food, it might be best if he didn't do it all at once. Now he was too full for dessert.

"Don't anyone leave the table yet," Mom said after their meal was over and the dishes had been cleared away. "It's time for Grandma to open her presents, and then we'll have cake and ice cream."

Grandma smiled as Mom handed her the gifts. "You didn't need to get me anything. Just having you all here is gift enough for me."

"We're glad we could be here," Mom said, "but we wanted to give you something."

Everyone nodded in agreement.

As Grandma opened her gifts, she smiled and commented on each one. When she got to the framed wildflower design Mattie had made, she smiled and said, "Danki, Mattie. I can see you worked hard making this for me." Then she mouthed the words, "I love you, too," to Mattie. "Maybe you can explain to me later how you dried the wildflowers."

Mattie smiled. She was glad Grandma liked what she had created with the flowers.

"I'm going to get Grandma's birthday cake now." Mom moved over to the counter and came back with a huge chocolate cake. It had been decorated with creamy white frosting and red flowers that looked like real roses.

"This looks *appeditlich*," Grandma said when Mom placed the birthday cake in front of her. "Why, it's almost too pretty to eat."

"I made it to eat, and Mattie helped me decorate it," Mom said as she lit the candles on the cake. "Now, let's sing 'Happy Birthday' to Grandma, and then she can blow out her candles and make a wish."

"I really don't know what to wish for," Grandma said. "I'm with my family tonight, so I have everything I want right here in this room."

Grandpa gave a nod. "Same goes for me."

"You can blow out your candles even if you don't make a wish," Mattie said.

Everyone sang "Happy Birthday," and when the song ended, Grandma leaned close to the candles and blew. All the candles went out except one. She blew on it again, but it stayed lit. Twice more Grandma blew, although it did no good. That one lone candle continued to flicker.

"All right," she said, squinting her eyes at Grandpa. "Are you the practical joker who put a trick candle on my cake?"

Grandpa's cheeks turned bright red as he leaned his head back and laughed. Everyone else joined in. Mattie thought it was pretty funny, until Grandpa's false teeth shot out of his mouth and landed on his plate with a *clink!* Everyone laughed even harder after that— everyone but Mattie, that is. Seeing Grandpa without any teeth in his mouth, and with his lips kind of sunken, caused Mattie to worry. What if she lost all her teeth and had to get dentures? That would be much worse than being short like Mark.

"What's the matter, little *bruder*?" Ike teased Mark as they all sat around the bonfire Grandpa had started in the backyard. "You only had a little piece of cake for dessert and no ice cream at all. Did you eat too much for supper?"

"Jah, I did." Mark held his belly, feeling annoyed at his brother for mentioning food. Mark loved chocolate cake and wanted to eat more, but his stomach was so full he thought it might burst. Now here they were, two hours later, and he wasn't sure he'd be able to enjoy the marshmallows the rest of the family had started roasting.

"Be careful now, son," Dad warned when Perry got

too close to the flames.

Perry stepped away from the fire, and Mom gave him and little Ada each a marshmallow. That seemed to make them both happy, as they handed them to Dad to roast.

"I like my marshmallows to catch on fire so the outside turns black." Calvin smiled, showing evidence of ash between his teeth from the marshmallow he'd just eaten.

"Me, too," Russell agreed, waving a flaming marshmallow back and forth with his stick.

"You all need to watch out that you don't burn your fingers or mouths," Mom warned. "Those marshmallows can get hot real quick when they start melting."

Grandpa had a nice fire going by then, and the warmth from it felt good as the night air started to chill. He also kept a hose nearby, which he always did whenever they had a campfire. Every now and then he'd wet the grassy area around the burning branches so the fire wouldn't spread any farther than it should.

"Here comes Grandma with some hot chocolate." Grandpa grinned, running over to assist her with the thermos, mugs, graham crackers, and chocolate bars for s'mores. Suddenly, the hose got wrapped around his foot, and down he went with a *thud!*

"Grandpa, are you all right?" Mark yelled, forgetting that his stomach still hurt.

Dad and Ike hurried over to help Grandpa to his

feet. Then they held on to him as they moved over to
one of the lawn chairs.

"I—I think I'm okay. Just need to catch my breath
is all." Grandpa panted, taking a seat. "Guess I didn't
realize the hose was around my foot. Don't think I broke
anything or pulled any muscles, though. It just knocked
the wind out of me."

"Maybe we'd better go inside," Mom said, kneeling
down next to her father with a look of concern.

"Are you kidding me?" Grandpa took Grandma's
shaky hand. She was obviously quite upset. "Your
grandma and I have been looking forward to this all week,
and nothing's going to ruin her birthday celebration. And
don't you worry, 'cause I'm really not hurt."

Everyone sighed with relief—especially Grandma,
whose sigh was the loudest.

What if Grandpa had been seriously hurt? Mark
wondered. *I hope there's nothing else in the yard that
could cause an accident.* Mark thought about the time
Grandma Miller had gotten some food caught in her
throat and how a teenage boy had saved her by using
the Heimlich maneuver. Last month Grandpa Miller
had gotten a book showing how to do the maneuver that
could dislodge something that was stuck in a person's
throat. He'd taught Mark and the rest of the family how
to do it, as well.

Mark might be little, but he wanted to know all
he could about helping his family and friends in an

emergency, because one never knew when a situation like that could arise.

While the rest of the family went back to having fun, enjoying hot chocolate, and making s'mores, Mark took the hose, straightened it out, and moved it away from where everyone sat. After that, he made a quick jaunt around the backyard to make sure there was nothing else that could cause another accidental fall. Seeing Grandpa Troyer go down like that had caused Mark to worry it might happen to someone else. He was thankful Grandpa was okay.

CHAPTER 5

Mattie's Tooth

A week after the Millers returned home from Grandpa and Grandma Troyer's, one of Mattie's bottom teeth started to ache. It felt worse by the time she and Mark rode home from school on Monday afternoon.

Oh no, Mattie thought. *This can't be happening to me.*

"What's wrong, Mattie?" Mark called over his shoulder. "How come you're not pedaling anymore?"

"I'm worried," she replied, rolling her tongue over her throbbing tooth.

"Again? What are ya worried about this time?"

"One of my teeth hurts." Mattie swallowed hard, trying hard not to cry.

"How long's it been hurtin'?" Mark asked.

"Off and on all day, but it's gotten worse since we left the schoolhouse. It's really aching right now, and I'm getting a headache."

"You'd better tell Mom as soon as we get home," Mark said. *"Zaahweh is schlechdi kumpani."*

Mattie sniffed. "I know a toothache is a bad companion,

and I can't help but be worried."

"Aw, don't worry, Mattie. Mom will take ya to the dentist, and he'll fix your tooth."

"What if he pulls it? I—I don't want to lose all my teeth and end up having to wear dentures like Grandpa Troyer does."

"Is it a permanent tooth?" Mark asked.

"No, I think it's one of my baby teeth," she replied.

"Then there's nothin' to worry about, 'cause even if the dentist does have to pull your tooth, another one will sooner or later grow in its place."

"Maybe so, but. . ."

"You weren't worried about losin' all your teeth and havin' to wear dentures when you lost some of your baby teeth before," Mark reminded Mattie.

"That's true, but that was before I saw Grandpa Troyer without all his teeth." Mattie sniffed, imagining what she would look like with no teeth in her mouth.

"You're not gonna lose all your teeth. The dentist will probably just drill a hole in your tooth and put a filling in." Mark glanced back at Mattie again. "You're not cryin', are ya?"

"A little bit," Mattie admitted with a sniff. She didn't want to be a baby about it, but it was hard not to cry.

"Well, there's nothin' to cry about. I'm sure you'll be okay."

"That's easy for you to say. You're not the one with a zaahweh."

"You're right, but I have lost some of my baby teeth, and I never worried about ending up with dentures." Mark laughed. "Remember the time Ike wanted to pull one of my top teeth 'cause it was loose?"

"Jah, and you wouldn't let him."

"That's because I wanted to pull it myself."

Mattie cringed, just thinking about the way Mark had grabbed hold of his tooth with a piece of tissue and given it a quick twist. He'd let out a yelp when the tooth popped out, and then he'd run for the bathroom to rinse out his mouth. Mattie had never pulled any of her baby teeth when they were loose. She'd just wiggled them a bit and let them fall out on their own. But this tooth was different. It wasn't loose, and unfortunately, it hurt really bad. Even so, she wanted to keep the tooth until it fell out on its own.

Forcing herself to think of something else, Mattie kept her legs pedaling as they neared home. She was glad when they finally arrived and she was able to get off the bike.

As soon as the twins put the bike away, Mark and Mattie hurried into the house. They found Mom in the kitchen, washing a head of lettuce at the sink.

"How was your day?" Mom asked, smiling as she turned to look at Mark and Mattie.

"It was okay," Mattie mumbled. She couldn't get up the nerve to tell Mom about her toothache. She just wanted to go to her room and have a good cry.

"Would you like a snack?" Mom asked, motioning to the table. "I baked some banana bread earlier today, and it's very good."

"No thanks," Mattie said. "I'm not hungerich right now."

Mom's eyebrows raised high on her forehead. "Now that's a first. Whenever you come home from school, you're always hungry and want something to eat."

"She doesn't want to eat 'cause she has a zaahweh," Mark blurted out.

"Is that true?" Mom asked, lifting Mattie's chin so she was looking into her eyes.

Mattie nodded slowly, and her chin began to quiver.

"How long's it been hurting?" Mom questioned.

"All day, but it got worse on the way home from school," Mattie admitted. Tears sprang to her eyes. "Oh Mom, I don't want to lose any of my teeth!"

Mom tipped her head. "What are you talking about, Mattie?"

"She's worried that if she goes to the dentist he might pull her tooth, and then she might end up with dentures like Grandpa Troyer," Mark spoke up.

"That's not going to happen," Mom said, pulling Mattie into her arms.

Mattie sniffed. "H–how did Grandpa lose all his teeth?"

"He didn't take good care of them when he was a boy, and from what I was told, by the time he was a young man he had to have them all pulled. Soon after that, he got a pair of false teeth. But they look really nice, and unless he takes them out, most people don't know they're not his real teeth." Mom gently patted Mattie's back. "I'm sure that won't happen to you, because you brush your teeth twice a day, and your *daed* and I make sure that you and all our *kinner* go to the dentist for regular checkups at least once a year."

Mattie knew Mom was probably right, but she was still worried about seeing the dentist, because she was afraid it might hurt.

"I'll go out to the phone shack right now and schedule a dental appointment for you. I'm sure Dr. Wallers will make your tooth feel better. But before I do that, let me take a look at that tooth." Mom turned quickly to Mark. "Would you please put the lettuce I was cleaning in the refrigerator? We're having salad with our supper tonight, and I want the lettuce to be nice and crisp."

"Sure, Mom," Mark said, taking the head of lettuce from her.

While he headed across the room to their propane refrigerator, Mom got out a flashlight and told Mattie to open her mouth real wide.

"It's this one," Mattie said, pointing to the tooth that was bothering her.

"Well," said Mom after taking a good look at Mattie's sore tooth, "I don't see any infection around the gum area, so it might only be a cavity. If that's the case, I'm sure the dentist can fix it real quick."

Mattie hoped that was true, but in spite of what Mom had said, she was still plenty worried.

As the family sat at the table having supper that evening, Mark felt bad seeing Mattie so upset. She'd only eaten a little of her food, and when she asked to be excused so she could go to her room, he was worried.

"Jah, you can go," Mom said, smiling at Mattie with a look of understanding.

"I'm sorry your tooth bothers you so much," Dad called as Mattie left her chair and slipped out of the room.

"Poor Mattie," Mom said, passing Dad the hamburger buns. "Her tooth is really hurting tonight, but I gave her an aspirin to help with the pain."

"Did you make Mattie a dental appointment?" Dad asked.

"Jah. I'll be taking her to see Dr. Wallers in the morning. The appointment is for ten o'clock."

"Does that mean Mattie won't have to go to school tomorrow?" Mark questioned, after he'd put lettuce, tomato, and a slice of pickle on his bun.

"That's right," Mom said. "She may be able to go after lunchtime, though."

"I'm not gonna ride the bike by myself." Mark

squirted some mustard, mayonnaise, and ketchup on his bun and then added another pickle. "I'd have to pedal twice as hard if I rode alone, and it's not as easy to steer when there's just one person."

"Why don't you walk to school?" Dad suggested. "It's not that far. Before you and Mattie got your bicycle built for two you used to walk all the time."

"That's true, but I like ridin' better than walkin'," Mark said.

"You can decide how you're going to get there when tomorrow comes." Mom motioned to Mark's plate. "Right now, you need to eat your supper."

Mark closed the lid on his bun and took a big bite. "Yum. This is sure good."

Dad looked at Mark strangely, and then he pointed to the only burger left on the platter Mom had placed on the table before they'd all sat down. "Mark, did you take a hamburger?"

"I—I think I did." Mark opened the lid on his bun and removed the lettuce, tomato, and two pickles. When he got to the bottom of the bun and discovered there was no hamburger there, he snickered. "Guess I must've forgotten about the burger."

Dad leaned his head back and laughed so hard there were tears running down his cheeks. "I think you had so much stuff on that bun that you didn't even notice the meat was missing." He forked the burger off the platter and plunked it on Mark's plate.

Mark looked at Dad and grinned. "Danki. I'm sure it'll taste even better now."

"I should think so," said Mom.

Mark ate every bite on his plate, but he didn't eat too much, like he had when they'd gone to Grandma and Grandpa Troyer's for the birthday party. He didn't want to end up with another stomachache. He'd realized since then that eating more food wouldn't help him grow any faster. He'd just have to be patient and wait until he caught up to Mattie. After all, she wasn't that much taller than him—just a few inches. And so far, none of the kids at school had even mentioned his height.

When supper was over and Mark had been excused from the table, he hurried upstairs and knocked on Mattie's door. *Tap! Tap! Tap!*

"Come in," she said in a squeaky voice. Mark wondered if she might have been crying.

When Mark entered the room, he found Mattie sitting at the foot of her bed, rocking back and forth as she hugged one of her dolls to her chest. As he drew closer, he noticed tears in Mattie's eyes, so he knew for sure she had been crying.

"Are you okay?" he asked, feeling concern for his sister. "Want me to tickle your feet or tell ya a funny joke?"

She flapped her hand at him. "Go away, Mark. I'm not in the mood for tickling or joke telling right now."

"Sorry, Mattie. I was only tryin' to make ya feel better." Tickling or telling a funny joke was the best way

Mark knew of to cheer someone up. He guessed when people were in pain, like Mattie, they probably didn't want to be tickled, though.

"I'm not gonna feel one bit better till my tooth stops hurting," she said.

"Guess I'd feel the same way if my tooth ached," Mark commented, unsure of what else to say. He hated to see Mattie sitting there with tears in her eyes.

Just then, Mom stepped into the room, holding a small dish. "I hope you're not bothering your sister," she said, looking at Mark.

Mark shook his head. "I was tryin' to make her feel better."

Mom sat on the bed beside Mattie. "Is the aspirin I gave you earlier helping your toothache?"

Mattie nodded. "But I'm still worried about going to the dentist tomorrow."

Mom set the dish on the table by Mattie's bed and took Mattie's hand. "Let's pray and ask God to calm your fears. Then you can eat the strawberry yogurt I brought you. It'll go down easy and shouldn't hurt your tooth."

As Mom and Mattie bowed their heads, Mark closed his eyes, too. *Dear Lord,* he silently prayed, *please be with Mattie when she goes to the dentist tomorrow, and help her not to worry or be afraid.*

CHAPTER 6

Grandpa Miller's Advice

When Mattie woke up the following morning, her stomach felt queasy. She'd be going to the dentist today, and he would look at her tooth. She hoped that whatever he had to do to correct the problem wouldn't hurt.

I guess it can't hurt any more than it does right now, she thought, frowning as she touched her mouth.

Mattie hurried to get dressed and went downstairs, where she found Mom in the kitchen fixing scrambled eggs for breakfast.

"Guder mariye," Mom said. "How are you feeling this morning?"

"Good morning," Mattie replied. "My tooth still hurts, and I'm *naerfich* about going to the dentist."

Mom's forehead wrinkled. "I thought after our little talk last night, and then our time together in prayer, that you would feel better about things and wouldn't feel so nervous."

Mattie nodded. "I did then. But when I woke up, I felt naerfich all over again."

Mom patted Mattie's shoulder. "It's going to be all right. Try not to worry, Mattie."

Watching as Mom dished out some scrambled eggs for her, Mattie was glad they were soft and would be easy to eat. She liked ketchup on her eggs, so after shaking a little over them, she took her first bite. Her stomach growled noisily, and the sound was more pronounced than the knot she felt there.

Dad chuckled. "Hmm. . . Sounds like someone's hungerich this morning."

Mattie forced a smile and looked over at Mom. "Thanks for making me scrambled eggs. They taste good and don't hurt my tooth when I chew on that side."

"I'm glad," Mom said as she poured Mattie a glass of orange juice.

Mattie took a drink, hoping Mom was right about how things would go at the dentist's today. This good breakfast Mom had fixed seemed to help Mattie's nervous stomach. Still, she would be relieved when her appointment was over and the pain in her tooth was gone.

It seems weird going to school without Mattie, Mark thought as he trudged along the path that led to the schoolhouse, kicking at small rocks with the toe of his boot. He'd decided not to ride their bicycle built for two today, since it would be harder to pedal on his own. Since Russell and Calvin had their own bikes, they were way ahead of him, which was always the case anyway. Mark didn't care. He still had plenty of time to get there.

Mark had just entered the schoolyard when Mattie's friend Stella bounded up to him. "Where's Mattie?" she asked. "And how come you walked to school today instead of riding your bike?"

"Mattie has a zaahweh, so our *mamm* is taking her to see the dentist this morning," Mark replied.

Stella frowned. "That's too bad. She didn't say anything about her tooth hurting yesterday."

"Well, it did. By the time we got home from school, Mattie was almost in tears because it was throbbing so bad."

"I'm sorry to hear that. I hope everything goes well at the dentist for her," Stella said.

"I'm sure it will, but Mattie's worried that Dr. Wallers might have to pull her tooth." Mark shook his head. "Ever since we went to Burton for Grandma Troyer's birthday, Mattie has been worried that she might lose all of her teeth."

"Why would she think that?"

Mark told Stella about Grandpa Troyer's false teeth falling out and onto his plate when he'd laughed so hard at Grandma trying to blow out the trick candle on her birthday cake. "It was pretty funny to see Grandpa's teeth lyin' there like that," Mark added with a snicker. " 'Course Mattie didn't laugh, and now she's concerned that she might end up with dentures, too."

"If she takes good care of her teeth, she should have them for a long time," Stella said. "My mamm makes me brush my teeth twice a day—in the morning after breakfast, and at night before I go to bed."

Mark bobbed his head. "That's what everyone in our family does, too."

"How come your grandpa lost all his teeth?" Stella questioned.

Mark told her the details, and then he spotted his friend John, who'd just arrived at school. He was about to go talk to John when the school bell rang.

"Guess we'd better get inside," Stella said. "When you see Mattie, tell her I'm thinking of her."

"You can tell her yourself," Mark said. "She's supposed to be here later, after she's done at the dentist's."

As Mattie sat in the waiting room at the dentist's office, she tried to think of things to make herself relax. First she looked at a magazine, but that was boring. Then she looked out the window and counted the cars going by. After that, she worked on a puzzle that was set on a small table for kids to put together. It seemed like it was taking forever for her name to be called. She was about to ask Mom if she knew what was taking so long when the dentist's receptionist stepped out from behind the desk and walked up to them.

"I just spoke with Dr. Wallers on the phone," she said. "He had a flat tire on the way here, so he's going to be a little late." She looked at Mom. "Would you like to wait, or should I schedule another appointment for Mattie on a different day?"

Mom shook her head. "My daughter's tooth hurts, so she needs to see the dentist today. We'll just wait until he gets here."

Oh great, Mattie thought. *Now I have to worry and wait even longer.* She was glad her folks had a horse and buggy instead of a car. Although it did take longer to go places by horse and buggy, at least they would never end up with a flat tire.

Mark turned his head and glanced up at the battery-operated clock on the schoolhouse wall near the teacher's desk. It was almost two o'clock, and still no Mattie. He thought for sure that she would be here by now. *I wonder what's taking her so long. Did something bad happen at the dentist's this morning? What if he did have to pull Mattie's tooth? Oh, I hope that's not the case.*

By the time their teacher dismissed the class to go home, Mark was upset. Mattie hadn't come to school at all today, and he was even more worried. He wished he had his bicycle after all, so he could get home quicker to see what happened. But, then, having to pedal it alone would have made things go slower than usual. But maybe he could get home just as quick if he ran all the way.

Mark took off running as fast as his legs would go. Normally he was a slow runner, but not today. He needed to get home quickly and find out if Mattie was okay. He felt lucky that he'd never had a toothache. He could only imagine what his sister had gone through.

When Mark got home from school, he noticed that Calvin and Russell's bikes were parked near the barn. He figured they were either in there or had gone up to the house. As he approached the back door, Mark was surprised to see Mattie sitting on the porch blowing bubbles.

She smiled at him and said, "How was school today?"

"It was okay." Still out of breath from running so hard, Mark took a seat on the step beside her. He noticed that she talked kind of funny and her lip looked a bit crooked. "How was your dental appointment?" he asked.

"Fine. The dentist filled my tooth, and now it doesn't hurt anymore. Wanna see?" Mattie opened her mouth really wide.

Mark took a peek, and sure enough, right where she'd pointed was a shiny silver filling. "Wow, that's a big one!" he exclaimed.

"Since it's a baby tooth, I won't have the filling when the old tooth falls out and a new one comes in," Mattie explained.

"Did it hurt when the dentist filled your tooth?" Mark asked.

"Only a little when they numbed it up. After that, I didn't feel a thing." Mattie blew another bubble. "Dr. Wallers had it done in no time at all."

"That's good. I was worried when you didn't show up at school this afternoon. What happened? If it didn't take long, how come you didn't come to school?"

"The dentist arrived late because he had a flat tire on the way to his office," Mattie replied. "So my appointment ended up being later than expected. Afterward, Mom said there was no point in me goin' to school, since I'd only be there a couple of hours. So we went to Grandma and Grandpa Millers' to pick up Ada and Perry." Mattie smiled. "Mom invited them over here to join us for supper, and they're in the house right now."

Mark grinned. "That's good. I always like to see our grandparents."

Mark's cat, Lucky, leaped onto the porch and flopped onto her back. Mark leaned over and rubbed her belly. *Purr. . . Purr. . . Purr. . .* Lucky pawed at the air, as if begging for more. Mark reached down to pet her again, but this time she got up, lumbered across the porch, came back toward Mark, and flopped down once more.

"That cat is so spoiled," Mattie said.

"She just knows what she likes." Mark chuckled. "She's a plopper, that's what she is."

"You're right about that. Lucky likes to plop down and have her belly rubbed whenever she can."

"Know what, Mattie?" Mark asked, tipping his head while looking at Mattie.

"What?"

"You talk kinda funny." Mark snickered and pointed to Mattie's mouth. "And you're slobberin' a bit, too."

"That's 'cause my mouth is still sort of numb." She handed Mark the bottle of bubble solution and wiped her mouth on her sleeve. "Wanna blow a few bubbles?"

"Jah, sure." Mark took the bottle, stuck the wand inside, and blew a big bubble. He continued to do this and blew several more. Lucky caught sight of the bubbles and started chasing and batting at them. Mark's other cat, Boots, jumped down from the fence post where he'd been sitting and joined in on the bubble-chasing game.

Mark laughed. So did Mattie. It looked funny to see the cats trying to catch the bubbles. Every time they smacked a bubble with their paws, it would pop.

Then Mattie's dog, Twinkles, got in on the act. She zipped across the yard, leaped into the air, and snapped at the bubbles.

"I don't want Twinkles getting sick from those bubbles, so I'd better put her in the house." Mattie got up to open the back door. "C'mon, Twinkles. You need to go inside now."

Twinkles did as Mattie asked, and then Mattie

quickly shut the door.

"Don't know why you were worried about Twinkles getting sick. I'm not worried about my katze," Mark said. "Don't think a little soapy bubble solution will hurt 'em any."

Mattie shrugged. "Maybe not, but if I swallowed bubble solution, I'm sure it would make me feel sick to my stomach, so it's better for Twinkles to be in the house."

Mark continued to blow bubbles until both cats stopped and arched their backs, looking toward the side of the house. Boots jumped in the air and landed on top of Lucky. Then Lucky darted into the field on the other side of the fence.

Mark gulped when he saw a small red fox following close behind his cats.

"Oh no! Come back!" Mark jumped up from the porch step and dashed into the yard. But it was too late—his cats and the fox were already way out in the field.

"It's all my fault. I should have put the cats in the barn instead of letting 'em jump at the bubbles." Mark removed his straw hat and slapped it against his legs. "What if that fox gets my katze?"

"They were running pretty fast," Mattie said, joining Mark and putting her arm around his shoulders. "Maybe they'll jump onto the fence post or climb into a tree to get away from the fox."

Mark sniffed, trying hard not to give in to the tears stinging his eyes. "If anything happens to Boots or

Lucky, I'll be the one to blame."

"Here, here, what seems to be the matter?" Grandpa Miller asked, stepping out of the house and joining the twins on the lawn.

"Mark's katze got chased by a red fox, and he's worried that the fox is gonna get 'em," Mattie explained.

Grandpa motioned to the porch. "Come sit with me, and we'll see if we can figure this out." He lowered himself to the top step on the porch and winked at Mark, his blue eyes twinkling like fireflies on a hot summer night.

Once Mark and Mattie were seated on the porch, on both sides of Grandpa, he said, "Now the way I see it, maybe that old fox just wanted to give your cats a little exercise. You said it was a red fox, right?"

The twins nodded in agreement.

"I know that red foxes are pretty fast on their feet, and if that one wanted your cats, he would have had them, just like that." Grandpa snapped his fingers. "Why, I'll bet those cats are having as much fun with that fox as he is with them."

"Knowing Boots and Lucky, they're probably just out of reach, teasing the fox like they do Twinkles." Mattie looked over at Mark. "Right?"

"Maybe so," Mark said with a nod.

"See there, all that worry was for nothing." Grandpa smiled. "Hey, how about letting me try blowing some of those bubbles?"

Mark handed Grandpa the bottle of liquid, and Grandpa blew a large bubble. "See that?" he said, as the bubble floated above their heads.

"Jah," Mark and Mattie both said.

"Well, my daed used to have an old saying about worry and bubbles."

"What was that, Grandpa?" Mark asked.

"When someone in my family started to fret about something, Dad always said that worries were like bubbles—they'll soon blow away."

Mark rubbed the bridge of his nose as he thought about what Grandpa had said. He'd never thought about worry being compared to a bubble before. He was about to ask Grandpa if he thought that was really true when he caught sight of his two cats leaping through the tall grass. As they neared the barn, they raced through the open door.

"They're safe!" Mark and Mattie hollered at the same time.

Mark sighed with relief.

Secret Gifts

For the next several weeks, Mattie set her worries aside.
With the holidays in full swing, her spirits were lifted.
The air seemed like it was charged with excitement,
and she could hardly stop smiling. Thanksgiving had
been a wonderful time with her family around the table,
sharing a tasty meal. Mattie's favorite part had been
the turkey and moist stuffing, but the pumpkin and
apple pies were delicious, too. Now she looked forward
to Christmas, which was just three weeks away. Every
free moment, Mattie spent working on Christmas
presents for everyone in the family, like she was doing
today. Since it was Saturday and all of her chores were
finished, she'd gone upstairs to her room to work on
some of the gifts still needing to be done.

Mattie didn't have much money saved up, so she'd
decided to make all the gifts she'd be giving to others
this year. It was actually fun to create some neat things,
and she hoped everyone would like the secret gifts she
had made. So far, she'd created felt pouches for both

Grandpa and Grandma Miller to keep their glasses in. For Grandpa Troyer she'd taken an old ring-binder notebook, decorated it with fabric squares cut into a patchwork pattern and then glued to the binder. When Grandpa Troyer's arthritis wasn't acting up, he liked to work in the garden, so Mattie had added a gift tag that read: GRANDPA'S GARDENING NOTES. She'd also made a three-ring binder for Grandma Troyer and decorated it with light blue material, pieces of lace, and some strips of white ribbon. On Grandma's note tag Mattie had written the words: GRANDMA'S RECIPES. Since Grandma liked to cook a lot, Mattie thought she would enjoy having her own recipe book.

Using a piece of pink-colored felt, Mattie had made a special little case where Mom could keep her needles and pins. She'd decorated it with a red heart on the outside and a matching piece of red felt on the inside to stick the needles in. Mattie's gift for Dad was a small tin she'd gotten from Mom that used to have tea in it. Mattie had painted it and added the words: DAD'S KEYS. Since Dad often lost his keys, she thought this would be a good gift for him.

Recently, Mattie had finished three bait containers that could be used for fishing. She'd made them from empty coffee cans she had secretly hidden in her closet. She thought Calvin, Russell, and Ike would like how she'd painted the cans, using a different color, with their names on each one.

Using sheets of craft foam, Mattie had made several bath foam shapes for Ada and Perry. The ones for Ada she'd cut to look like flowers, and Perry's were shaped like fish. She was sure they would enjoy playing with them whenever they took a bath.

Mattie still had to finish gifts for Mark and her schoolteacher, Anna Ruth, but thankfully, she didn't have to decide what to make for her best friend, Stella. During the early days of autumn, Mattie had collected some pods that had fallen from a sweet gum tree along the route to school. With those, she'd created a little mouse, and it had turned out really cute. When making the mouse, Mattie had used a small acorn for the head, gluing it to the pod, which was the body for the mouse. She'd then applied different seeds she had found, using them for the eyes and ears. Luckily, the pod had a stem attached, and that was perfect for the tail. She had used some pine needles for whiskers and finished it off by gluing the mouse to a small piece of wood. It wasn't that hard to make and didn't take her long at all. It was a good thing she'd gathered all the materials, even though at the time she'd had no idea what she would use them for.

For her teacher, Mattie planned to make a felt and ribbon bookmark, using scraps of pink felt, red ribbon, and white buttons. She hoped everyone would like the gifts she'd made for them.

Mattie had just taken a seat at her desk to begin

working on Mark's secret gift when someone knocked on her bedroom door.

"Who is it?" Mattie called.

"It's me, Mark."

"You can't come in right now," Mattie said loudly. "I'm busy making Christmas gifts, and I don't want you to see what I'm working on for you."

Mark rapped on the door again. "If I can't come in, then would ya please come out in the hallway?"

"I'll be right there." Mattie set aside the aluminum pie pan and pile of rocks she'd placed on her desk, which she was going to use for Mark's garden plaque, and opened her bedroom door. When she stepped into the hallway, she was careful to block the door so her brother couldn't see in.

Mark held a small cellophane sack with a pine cone inside. "Take a whiff of this," he said, lifting it up to Mattie's nose. "I made this for Grandma Troyer. Do ya think she'll like it?"

Mattie sniffed deeply. "Umm. . . That smells appeditlich. What's in there to make it smell so delicious?"

"A pine cone, two cinnamon sticks, and a dried-out orange slice." He grinned, looking quite pleased with himself. "I made one for Grandma Miller, too."

"I'm sure they'll both like 'em to hang in the house, and it'll make whatever room they put it in smell real nice," Mattie said.

"Sure hope so." Mark put his hand on the knob of

Mattie's bedroom door. "What are you makin' in there?"

She wagged her finger back and forth. "You'll have to wait till Christmas to find out."

"Aw, Mattie, can't ya at least give me a hint?"

She shook her head. "It's supposed to be a surprise. Now please step away from my door. Don't you want to be surprised on Christmas?"

Mark's only reply was a quick shrug.

"It's no fun knowing ahead of time if you see what I'm going to give you."

He frowned. "You're no fun."

"I'm not tryin' to be fun. I'm busy."

"Wanna play a game?" he asked.

"Not right now."

"How about hide-and-seek?"

"No!" Mattie stepped back into her room and quickly shut the door. She figured if she played the game and hid from Mark, he'd sneak into her room and see what she was making for him, and it would spoil the surprise. Well, that wasn't going to happen. Mattie knew her twin brother well, so as soon as she finished making his gift, she would hide it in the back of her closet, along with all the other gifts she had made.

Mark snickered as he made his way down the hall to his room. Mattie could sure get riled easily. He'd only been teasing when he'd threatened to go in her room to see what she was making for him. Of course, he was curious to know, but he could wait until Christmas. Besides, he didn't want to spoil the surprise. In the meantime, he had some gifts he needed to finish for family members, too—including one for Mattie. He hoped she would like the surprise gift he was making, because he'd tried hard to come up with something different to give her.

Mark stepped into his room, shut the door, and walked over to the window. He saw his two cats below in the yard, jumping at a flower stem gently blowing in the late autumn breeze. Mark was glad Lucky and Boots had returned after being chased into the field by that red fox. Grandpa Miller had been right about Boots and Lucky being able to take care of themselves. Mark wished he could have known what had actually happened, but later that evening, watching from the porch, he couldn't help giggling when he saw his cats prancing around the yard, swishing their tails while holding their heads up high.

Going over to his desk, Mark looked at the gifts he'd already completed. He was happy with the way the wind chimes had turned out that he planned to give Mom and both of his grandmas for Christmas. He'd thought about giving them each a box of chocolates but had decided on the chimes instead. It was a good thing he liked to collect small and unusual rocks, because for the top of the wind chimes, he'd stained a small, round-shaped piece of wood he'd gotten from Dad's shop and then glued a few rocks to the top. After that, he'd attached to the wood some fishing line Grandpa Miller had given him. Mark had finished it off by hooking some of Mom's old spoons to the line. Those would cause the chimes to jingle whenever there was a breeze.

For Dad and both of his grandpas, Mark had thought about using some strips of craft foam to make soda pop can coolers. But since neither Dad nor his grandpas drank much soda pop, he'd changed his mind and painted some of the bigger stones in his collection to use as paperweights instead. He was glad most of the gifts were pretty much done, and now he was going to begin work on a pair of hand warmers for Calvin and Russell. They would be made from thick fabric sewed together in squares and filled with rice. To warm them, the boys would need to put them in the oven on low for a while, and if they stuck the hand warmers inside their jacket pockets when they went outside, their hands would be toasty warm.

Mark felt pretty good about the gifts he'd made so far, and he was just getting ready to fill Russell's hand warmer with rice when someone knocked on his door. *Tap! Tap! Tap!*

"Who is it?" Mark called.

"It's me—Calvin."

"What do ya want?"

"I want to ask you something."

Mark groaned. He figured Calvin would keep knocking if he didn't open the door.

"What do you want?" Mark asked when he stepped out of his room and closed the door behind him.

"I was wondering if you'd like to go for a bike ride with me and Russell," Calvin said.

Mark shook his head. "No thanks. I'm busy working on some Christmas presents, and so is Mattie. Anyways, it's too cold to go bike riding today."

"It's not that cold." Calvin peered around Mark toward the closed door. "What kind of gifts are you makin' in there?"

"I'm not tellin'," Mark said. "You'll have to wait till Christmas to find out."

Snow

On Christmas Eve day it started to snow, and Mattie began to worry all over again.

"What if the roads get bad and Grandpa and Grandma Troyer can't make it for Christmas?" Mattie asked Mom as she stared out the living room window, watching the snowflakes increase by the minute.

"Now don't start fretting, because it won't change a thing," Mom said with a click of her tongue. "Why don't you go find somethin' to do? If you keep busy, it'll take your mind off the weather."

"That's right," Dad spoke up from his chair across the room. "Blessed is the person who is too busy to worry in the daytime and too sleepy to worry at night."

"Maybe Dad's right," Mark said, joining Mattie at the window. "Why don't we find somethin' to do?"

"Like what?" Mattie wanted to know.

"We can play a game of checkers."

She shook her head. "You always win when we play that game. Let's put a puzzle together instead."

"No way," Mark said. "The last time we did that, you kept out one of the pieces so you'd be able to put it in last."

Mattie turned her hands upward. "What can we do then?"

"Let's go out and play in the *schnee*," Mark suggested. "The way it's comin' down out there, I'll bet we could have a snowman built in no time at all."

That sounded like a good idea to Mattie, so she smiled and said, "I'll get my jacket, gloves, and scarf. Then we'll meet in the yard."

"Don't forget your rubber boots," Mom called as Mattie started out of the room.

"I won't," Mattie hollered over her shoulder, eager to do something other than worry.

By the time Mattie came outside, Mark already had a pretty good-sized snowball made. "What took ya so long?" he asked when Mattie joined him in the yard, which was now a blanket of white, with several inches of snow on the ground. "I thought maybe you'd changed your mind about helpin' me build a snowman."

"I couldn't find my rubber schtiffel," Mattie explained. "They were way in the back of my closet, behind all the Christmas presents I made. Sure didn't want to play in the snow without boots on my feet." Mattie was also glad for the wool scarf she wore on her head. It helped to keep her ears nice and warm.

Mark crunched through the snow until he was standing face-to-face with Mattie. "Wanna play hide-and-seek or tag or have a snowball fight?"

She wrinkled her nose. " 'Course not. I came out here to make a snowman, and so did you."

"I know, but we can build the snowman and then play a game."

Mattie shook her head. "I don't think so."

"Why not?" Mark gave her arm a little poke.

" 'Cause I don't want to. Besides, you know it's more fun to play hide-and-seek in the summer when it's warm outside."

"Dad said you should keep busy so you won't worry about the weather," Mark reminded Mattie.

"Jah, I know." She stood for a moment, watching Twinkles as she romped around in the snow. All dogs seemed to like the snow, and her dog especially did. Mark's cats didn't like the snow. They preferred to snuggle together on a bale of straw inside the barn, out of the cold.

It was fun to watch Twinkles jump from one point to another and then bury her little nose deep in the snow. Each time the dog would look up, she'd sneeze, sending the soft crystal flakes, which were stuck on the end of her nose, flying in every direction.

"Okay now, let's get the snowman done, and then we can decide what we want to do after that," Mark suggested.

"Okay." Mattie bent down and formed a snowball. She had the urge to throw it at her brother but knew if she did, he'd probably throw a bigger one at her, and then she'd have to throw another one at him. Pretty soon they'd have so much fun tossing snowballs that they'd never get the snowman done. So Mattie began rolling the snowball around the yard until it grew bigger and bigger. Mark did the same with the snowball he had started. Soon the twins had three good-sized snowballs finished and stacked on top of each other.

"The snowman looks great! Isn't this fun?" Mark asked, patting some snow on the middle section to make some arms and fill in the gaps where more snow was needed.

Mattie nodded and glanced toward the road. "Shouldn't Grandma and Grandpa Troyer be here by now?"

Mark shrugged. "I don't know. Guess that all depends on what time they left Burton."

"I sure hope the guy bringing them to our house drives safe." Mattie sighed, putting her hands on top of her head. "I know Dad said not to, but I'm gonna worry till they get here. I haven't forgotten the accident we saw on the trip we made to celebrate Grandma's birthday. That accident was due to all the rain that had fallen, and snow is even worse."

"Worry if you must," Mark said, "but I'm gonna enjoy playin' in the snow." He slipped and slid across the yard, laughing as he went. When he got to Mom's garden, he bent down, pushed some snow aside, and found two small rocks. "I think these will work fine for the snowman's eyes!" he hollered to Mattie.

Losing interest in the snowman, Mattie stared at the driveway. She knew worrying would not bring Grandma and Grandpa here any sooner, but she just couldn't seem to help herself.

Mark and Mattie were getting ready to go back inside when a car pulled in, and Grandpa and Grandma Troyer got out.

"Good, they're here!" Mattie shouted. She tromped through the snow, and as soon as their grandparents got out of the vehicle, she gave them both a big hug. "I was getting worried and thought you'd never get here."

Grandma patted Mattie's shoulder, and she and Grandpa waved good-bye to their driver as he pulled out of the driveway. "We got a late start because our driver had an errand to run before he picked us up. But we're here now, safe and sound."

"What's in there?" Mark asked, pointing to the cardboard box in Grandpa's hands.

"Well, let's see now. . . There's Christmas presents, a few jars of cinnamon applesauce, and some of your grandma's delicious fudge." Grandpa smiled and winked at the twins. "And there might even be a few fritters for us to heat up later on."

Mark smacked his lips. "Yum! Nobody makes corn fritters like Grandma Troyer."

As they walked past the snowman, Grandpa stopped and asked if the twins had made it.

"We sure did," Mark said with a nod.

"You did a fine job, but I think the snowman needs a little something else." Grandpa removed the scarf from around his neck and draped it on the snowman. "There, how's that look?"

"It completes the snowman," Mark said, grinning up at Grandpa.

"I agree," said Mattie. She took Grandma's hand, and they all headed inside, where they were greeted by Mom, Dad, Ada, Perry, Calvin, Russell, and Ike.

"It's so good to see you," Mom said, giving her parents a hug.

"It's nice to see you, and I'm sorry we're so late," Grandma said. "I hope we didn't hold up supper tonight."

Dad shook his head. "My folks aren't here yet, so we'll wait awhile before we start eating."

Mom glanced at the clock above the fireplace. "They really should have been here by now."

"You're right," Dad agreed. "I wonder what could be taking them so long. They don't live that far away, and I figured they'd be here long before this."

"Maybe you should go over to their house and see if something's happened," Mom suggested. There was a worried frown on her face. "They might have run into a problem and need help with something."

Dad gave a nod. "That's a good idea. I'll hitch my horse to the buggy and go over there right now." He looked at Ike, who'd been standing near the fireplace warming his hands because he'd just come in from the barn after feeding the horses. "I'd like you to go with me, son," Dad said.

"Sure, okay. I'll get my jacket and stocking cap, and we can be on our way." Ike hurried out of the room, and Dad followed.

Mattie wished she could have gone, too. She was really worried now. What could be keeping Grandpa and Grandma Miller? Was there a problem with their horse or buggy? Did someone get sick? Oh, she hoped nothing had happened.

Since their other grandparents had just arrived, the rest of the family visited with Grandpa and Grandma Troyer and got caught up on what they'd been doing lately. Grandma said she'd been busy baking a lot of goodies for the holidays, and Grandpa said he'd been busy making several Christmas presents.

"Hey, we heard you got a new filling in your tooth," Grandpa said to Mattie. "Can I take a peek in there?" he asked, leaning close to her face.

"I had a bad toothache, but the dentist put a filling in it." Mattie opened her mouth so Grandpa could see. "It didn't hurt much at all."

"I'm glad to hear that," Grandpa said, peering at Mattie's mouth.

"That's because they numbed up her tooth," Mark piped up.

"I guess we can be thankful that nothing more serious has gone on since the last we saw you," Grandpa said, giving Mattie and Mark an extra hug. "Thankfully I haven't had any more falls since that hose wrapped around my foot, either."

"I'm happy to hear that," Mark said.

Mattie nodded in agreement.

After they had visited awhile longer, Mom and Grandma excused themselves and headed for the kitchen to check on the meal and heat up the fritters they would also have with supper. Meanwhile, Grandpa listened to what Calvin and Russell had been up to lately.

Mattie excused herself and went upstairs to her room. Going to the window, she couldn't believe how hard it was snowing. She loved having snow for Christmas but wished it hadn't started snowing until everyone arrived safely. *I hope Dad and Ike will be okay,* she thought, pressing her nose to the glass.

Now Mattie was really worried. She not only feared for Grandma and Grandpa Miller but also for her dad and oldest brother.

Please, God, take care of Dad and Ike, as well as Grandpa and Grandma Miller, she silently prayed. *And thank You for bringing Grandpa and Grandma Troyer safely here.*

Mattie hoped her prayers would make it all the way up through the snow to heaven. Closing her bedroom door, she went back downstairs to be with the family while she tried to leave her worries behind.

While they waited, Mark suggested they play a game with Ada and Perry. They'd just taken seats around the kitchen table to play Chutes and Ladders when Mattie heard sirens in the distance. She shivered. *Oh no. Could Grandpa and Grandma Miller have been in an accident?*

CHAPTER 9

Thinking Alike

"It's your turn now, Mattie. Quit daydreaming and play the game." Mark gave his sister's arm a nudge.

"I'm not daydreaming," Mattie said. "I was thinking about Grandma and Grandpa Miller."

"I'll bet you're worrying again," Mark said.

"I can't help it. If Grandpa and Grandma Troyer made it all the way from Burton with so much snow comin' down, then Grandpa and Grandma Miller should have been here hours ago." Tears welled in Mattie's eyes. "I just know something bad must have happened, especially since Dad and Ike aren't back yet, either."

"You don't know that," Grandma Troyer said, joining Mark and Mattie at the table where they sat with Ada and Perry. "Have you ever heard the old saying, 'No news is good news'?"

Mattie shook her head.

"Well, until we know why your other grandparents aren't here, there's no reason to worry." She gave Mattie's shoulder a gentle squeeze. "It might be something really simple, you know."

"Like what?" Mattie asked, looking up at Grandma, hoping to hear some comforting words.

"I'm not sure," Grandma said. "Maybe they got busy doing chores and lost track of time."

"That could be," Mark spoke up. "I remember one time last summer when Grandpa Miller was supposed to pick me up to go fishing, he got busy workin' on a crossword puzzle and wasn't watching the clock. By the time he remembered and came to pick me up, it was time for me to do my evening chores."

"Did you have to cancel the fishing trip?" Grandma asked.

Mark shook his head. "Nope. Grandpa helped me finish my chores, and then we went fishin'. Since it was summertime and didn't get dark till late, we had plenty of time to fish before I had to go home and get ready for bed."

Mattie's face relaxed a bit. "Maybe that's what happened today. Grandpa might have started working on another crossword puzzle."

"You could be right," Mark said. "Or maybe Grandma got busy working on one of her quilts."

"You know, children, worry is sort of like a rocking chair," Grandpa Troyer called from across the room, where he sat on the sofa with Perry and Ada on either side of him. "It gives you something to do but doesn't take you anywhere."

Mark and Mattie looked at each other and snickered. Sometimes Grandpa had an unusual way of saying things.

Just then, Mark heard the whinny of a horse. He jumped up and raced over to the window. Mattie did the same.

"They're here!" she shouted, jumping up and down when she saw Grandma and Grandpa Miller climb out of Dad's buggy.

The whole family rushed to the door and greeted them as soon as they stepped inside.

"Are you both okay?"

"Where have you been?"

"How come you're so late?"

Everyone spoke at once, bombarding Grandma and Grandpa with questions, until Grandpa Miller held up his hand and said, "One question at a time, please."

"Are you all right?" Mom asked.

Grandpa nodded and gave Grandma a sly little grin. "We both sat down to read a book this afternoon and ended up falling asleep."

"I guess we were more tired than we realized," Grandma Miller said. "We're glad our son came to get us, because if he hadn't, we might have slept right through the night." Her forehead wrinkled. "We'd have been very disappointed if we'd awakened in the morning and realized we'd missed spending Christmas Eve with our family."

"You're here now, and that's all that matters," Mom said, giving Grandma a hug.

Mark put his arm across Mattie's shoulders. "See, you were worried for nothing."

Mattie nodded. She was glad all four of their grandparents were here. Now, without worry, she was ready to celebrate Christmas.

The following morning after breakfast, everyone was ready to open their Christmas presents. Grandma and Grandpa Troyer had spent the night, and so had Grandma and Grandpa Miller. Now everyone was gathered in the living room to exchange gifts.

Mark was pleased when Mom and Dad gave him a fluorescent vest to wear whenever he rode his bike or had to walk along the side of the road. Mattie got one, too, and so did Calvin and Russell.

"It will make you more visible to drivers and keep you safe when you're walking near the road," Dad said.

"What does *visible* mean?" Mattie asked.

"Noticeable," Mark was quick to say. "That way cars can see us better."

All the children received some kind of toy or game from their grandparents, and Mark was especially pleased with the puzzle that had pictures of cats, which he'd received from Grandpa and Grandma Miller. It was supposed to glow in the dark after it was put together, and he could hardly wait to see that.

Mattie got a small loom for making pot holders, and they both received a new pair of gloves Grandma Troyer had knitted with soft but warm yarn. Mattie's gloves were blue and Mark's were brown. Those would definitely keep their hands from getting cold during the winter months. And even though the twins already owned a pair of gloves, it was always good to have a spare. Besides, the ones Grandma had made them were much nicer than their store-bought gloves.

The whole household was alive with energy, and everyone smiled when Ada and Perry opened up the stick horses Mom had made for them, using old broom handles and dark material from a pair of Dad's old trousers. She'd also used some yellow yarn for the horses' manes and felt cutouts for their eyes. A rope halter had been sewed at the end of each of the horses' heads so the children would have reins to hold on to while they pretended to ride their horses.

Ike surprised Mark with a ceramic plate, normally used to put under a flowerpot to keep the water from seeping out. This plate was green, and Ike told Mark he thought it would make a good pool to put near the frog house in Mattie's small garden. Mark couldn't agree more. Come springtime, his frog would have its very own pond.

Ike had also given Mom and both grandmas a box of chocolates, so Mark was glad he'd made them each some wind chimes instead.

Everyone seemed to like what Mark and Mattie had given them, too, and Mom said she was amazed at how creative each of the twins' gifts had been. "You both put a lot of time and effort into these gifts you made for each of us," she said, giving Mark and Mattie a tender squeeze.

"Jah," Grandma Troyer agreed, wiping a tear from her cheek. "We'll certainly treasure what we received from everyone today."

Now it was time for the twins to exchange gifts with each other, while the rest of the family looked on.

"Here ya go." Mark handed Mattie her present.

"And here you go," she said, giving Mark the gift she'd made for him.

Mark was surprised when he pulled out a garden plaque made from plaster of paris with rocks of various sizes and some colorful marbles stuck around the outer edges. "That's exactly what I made for you," he said, pointing at Mattie's gift as she removed it from the paper sack.

She giggled. "I guess we were thinking alike on these two gifts."

"Great minds think alike," Dad said with a smile.

Mark turned to Mattie and said, "Maybe we can put our plaques in your little garden near the frog pool. We can either lay them in the dirt or prop them up with a large rock behind 'em."

Mattie smiled. "That's a good idea, Mark."

"Why don't we sing a few Christmas carols now?" Grandma Miller suggested. "Christmas wouldn't be the same without carols."

Everyone nodded at that.

The first song the family sang was "Joy to the World." Mark smiled to himself, thinking about the joy of Jesus' birth. When the baby Jesus was born in Bethlehem all those years ago, He was God's gift to everyone in the world.

That night, as Mattie lay in her warm, comfortable bed, with a smile on her face, she thought about this wonderful day. Even though it had started out with many worries, the day ended up being practically perfect.

Both grandparents had arrived safely; they'd had lots of good food to enjoy together; everyone liked the gifts she and Mark had made; and they'd even had a white Christmas.

Once again, Mattie had been worried for nothing, and she knew she should have put her trust in the Lord.

Thank You, dear Jesus, Mattie prayed, *for giving us a wonderful Christmas and for keeping my family safe. Thank You for blessing us with the beautiful snow, and please keep everyone safe in their travels tomorrow. Most of all, dear Jesus, thank You for today, when we celebrate Your birthday.*

Mattie's eyelids grew heavier as she thought about all her gifts. Each one was special in every way. She was even excited about the ceramic plate Ike had given Mark for his frog. Mattie knew that Mark's frog would enjoy keeping cool in the water during the hot summer days. She also thought maybe some of the birds that came into the yard might like getting a drink or taking a bath in that little pool. Many times on the way to school, she and Mark had seen birds splashing around in puddles along the road after a heavy rainfall. She figured they might do the same thing in Mark's little frog pool.

As Mattie's eyes finally shut, her last thought was about what kind of flowers she would plant around the frog pool to give it some shade. Maybe she'd put in a small shrub or several of her favorite flowers. In any case, it would be wonderful to have something to look forward to in the spring.

Today was so much fun, Mark thought as he lay in bed. He felt good about how wonderful the day had turned out.

Mark listened to his parents and grandparents visiting downstairs. Their muffled voices and joyous laughter matched his own feelings as he fluffed up his pillow and snuggled under the covers.

Mark liked all the gifts he'd received today and was glad everyone liked what he'd made them, too.

Grandpa Miller had surprised Mark and Mattie when he'd given them two straws with a long piece of string put through the end of each one, along with a bottle of homemade bubble solution. Grandpa had shown them how to make huge bubbles with this simple creation.

After all the gifts had been opened, everyone had gone out to the porch to watch Mark and Mattie dip their straws and string into the soapy water, and then stretching each straw, and making the string really tight, they'd waved it in the air, creating huge bubbles. They were the largest ones Mark had ever seen. He and Mattie had fun seeing who could make the biggest bubbles. Everyone had been quite impressed when Mark made a bubble that looked like a caterpillar, with one big bubble and a bunch of smaller ones attached. The funny thing was, Mark hadn't even been trying to do that. It had just happened.

Mark snickered, reflecting more on Grandpa Miller's simple but fun gift. His two cats and Mattie's dog had enjoyed jumping up at the bubbles and making them pop.

Mark thought some more about how this night had ended. Before going to bed, he'd looked out his bedroom window and realized it had stopped snowing. Then he'd looked up and seen a beautiful, bright star among the smaller ones that filled the night sky like sparkling diamonds.

"I'll bet that was the Christmas star," Mark whispered, snuggling deeper into his pillow. "I wonder if that could have been the very same star in the Bible days that guided the three wise men to the place where Jesus was."

As Mark grew tired and more relaxed, he pictured the star in his head and was reminded of what today was really all about. Before falling asleep, he whispered a prayer. "Thank You, Lord Jesus, for blessing us in every way, not only today but all year long."

CHAPTER 10

Misunderstandings

"Can we make some pumpkin kichlin this morning?" Mattie asked her mother one Saturday in January.

"Not today," Mom said. "I'm taking Ada and Perry to the Shoe and Boot Store in Charm. Their feet have grown, and they need new winter boots."

"How about when you get back? Could we bake the cookies then?" Mattie asked.

Mom shook her head. "I'm sorry, Mattie, but I need to clean Ada's room this afternoon. After that, I'll be taking Ada and Perry over to Grandma Miller's so I can help her clean house."

"So Ada and Perry will be spending the whole day with you?"

Mom gave a nod.

Mattie frowned. "What am I supposed to do here all day by myself?"

"You won't be alone. Calvin and Russell will be at home, and your daed and Ike are out in the wood shop, so if you need anything, just let them know."

Mom patted Mattie's arm. "You can do whatever you want while I'm gone. Just don't try to do any baking. It wouldn't be safe for you to turn the oven on when no grown-ups are in the house."

"I won't," Mattie promised. She wished she was older and could turn the oven on by herself. She wished Mom wasn't too busy to help her bake cookies. She wished Mom would spend time with her today instead of with Ada and Perry.

Even though Mattie knew it wasn't really true, a little voice put a thought in her head. *I wonder if Mom loves Ada and Perry more than she loves me,* Mattie thought as she ambled out of the kitchen and tromped up the stairs to her room. *She didn't ask if I wanted to go with them to the Shoe and Boot Store, or even to Grandma Miller's house. I'll bet she'd rather spend the day with my little sister and brother instead of me.*

Mark took his sled from the barn, eager to try it out now that there was plenty of snow on the ground. First, though, he was going over to his friend John's to see if he'd like to go sledding. Mom had said it was okay for him to go, so he grabbed the rope on his sled and headed down the path toward his best friend's house.

Sure hope John's able to go sledding with me, Mark thought as he tromped through the snow in his rubber boots. He'd made sure to wear his new vest, too, so he could be seen easily by any cars going by. Now that the weather was colder, Mark didn't wear his straw hat anymore. Instead, he wore a knitted stocking cap on his head. On Sundays, though, when he dressed up for church, Mark wore a black felt hat, just like Dad and his brothers.

When Mark arrived at the Schrocks' house a short time later, he found John playing on his rope swing in the barn.

"Would ya like to go sledding with me?" Mark asked. "I'm goin' over to that big hill behind our neighbor's house."

"Sorry, but I can't go with ya today," John said, hopping off the swing with a grunt.

"How come?"

"Allen Hostetler's comin' over. I'll be visiting with him while our mothers do some sewing." John grinned. "When he gets here, I'm gonna ask if he wants to take turns swinging on the rope."

Mark frowned. "I was hoping you could go sledding. It would be a lot of fun."

"Maybe some other time," John said.

"Okay. See ya later then." With a feeling of disappointment weighing him down, Mark left the barn and headed out the driveway, wondering if John liked Allen better than him.

Holding tightly to the rope on his sled, Mark tromped all the way back home through the snow.

When he got there, he found Mattie on the front porch brushing her dog.

"Wanna go sledding with me?" Mark asked as he approached the house.

Mattie looked at him strangely. "I thought you were going with John."

"I was hoping for that, but he'll be visiting with Allen Hostetler today." Mark stepped onto the porch. "I need someone to go with me, because it wouldn't be any fun to sled alone."

Mattie motioned to her dog. "I'm busy with Twinkles right now."

"Can't ya do that some other time? Come on, Mattie, please go with me. The schnee is just right, and I wanna do some sleddin' before the weather turns warm and all the snow melts away. Go get your sled and come on. Time's a-wasting."

"Oh, all right," she finally agreed. "But only for a little while. I want to spend some more time with Twinkles today."

"You need to walk faster or your feet will get cold!" Mark hollered to Mattie as they trudged along the snowy path leading to their neighbor's hill.

"It's hard to walk in these rubber schtiffel I'm wearing when the snow's so deep," Mattie panted. "Sure wish I had a pair of snowshoes like Ike owns."

"Well, just keep walking, 'cause we're almost there." Mark pointed to the hill up ahead. Mattie huffed and puffed until they were finally at the top, and then she stopped walking and took a deep breath. "Can I ask you a question, Mark?"

"Sure. What do you want to know?"

"Do you think Mom loves Ada and Perry more than she loves me?"

Mark scrunched up his nose and looked at Mattie like she'd said something really strange. "Now why would ya ask me somethin' like that?"

"Mom spends a lot of time with Ada and Perry, just like she's doing today," Mattie said.

"They're little. They need more attention, and Mom needs to be around 'em more."

"I know, but I think Mom would rather be with them more than me."

Mark gave his stocking cap a tug. "I doubt that's the case, but I do believe that John Schrock would rather be with Allen instead of me."

"How do you know?" Mattie asked.

"If he liked me better, he'd be here sledding right now. I'm worried that I might have lost my best friend."

"You still have me," Mattie said. "I'll always be your twin sister and also your friend."

"I appreciate that, and you're my friend, too." Mark seated himself on his sled. "Now I think the two of us should start havin' some fun!"

Mattie jumped on her sled and raced Mark down the hill.

"I won!" he hollered when they reached the bottom.

"I don't care. It was fun just the same," Mattie said as she began pulling her sled back up the hill.

The twins continued to sled for a while, until Mattie's sled veered off course and jammed into a snowbank. She ended up with a face full of snow! "That's it for me," she said, spitting snow out of her mouth while shaking her head. "I'm cold and wet, and now all my teeth hurt from that icy schnee. I want to go home!"

"You're not hurt, are ya, Mattie?"

"No, but I have schnee in my schtiffel. When my feet are cold, the rest of me is chilled to the bone." She jumped up and down a few times. "Think my toes will be numb till I get home."

"Don't go yet, Mattie," Mark pleaded. "We haven't been here that long, and I want to sled some more. If you have snow in your boots, take 'em off and dump it out."

Mattie frowned and shook her head. "If I take my schtiffel off, then my stocking feet will get wet while I'm standing there trying to dump out the snow."

"You can sit on your sled to take off your boots. Besides, if you've got snow in the boots, then your feet are already wet."

"That's right," she said with a nod. "And that's exactly why I don't want to sled anymore. I wanna go home where it's nice and warm."

"Go right ahead then," Mark mumbled. "I'll just stay here and sled by myself."

Mattie hesitated a moment, and then she bent down and brushed the snow off her sled. "I'll see you at home, Mark." She grabbed the sled's rope and started pulling it down the hill toward home.

Mark groaned as he took a handful of snow and tasted it. He was disappointed that Mattie didn't want to be with him. She was still his twin sister, but maybe she wasn't his friend. He thought a true friend would have stayed and done more sledding with him.

He watched as Mattie departed and then frowned when she looked back at him and yelled, "You'd better not eat any more of that snow. It could be dirty, and it might make ya sick!"

"You should have ridden your sled back down the hill," Mark hollered, ignoring her comment. "It'd be a lot faster than walkin'."

Maybe I should head for home, too, Mark thought, shaking his head. *It won't be any fun staying here by myself.*

He was about to make one last trip down the hill on his sled when he spotted John and Allen coming toward him, each pulling a sled. From where Mark stood, watching as they approached, he could see their breath as they huffed and puffed. He also noticed that their cheeks were rosy as they made their way up the hill.

Mark figured by now, from the snow's chilling cold, that his cheeks were probably as red as theirs.

"We decided to join you," John called as they got closer to Mark. "Is that all right?"

Mark was tempted to say no at first but changed his mind. He decided that the three of them could maybe have a good time. He might have been worried for nothing. John was still Mark's friend, and Mark could be friends with Allen now, too.

When Mattie got home, she went straight to her room and changed into a clean, dry dress. Then she curled up on her bed, pulled a quilt up to her chin, and closed her eyes. Oh, how she wished she and Mom could have done some baking today. It would have been more fun than going sledding with Mark and getting cold and wet. She was also hungry for some pumpkin cookies. Just thinking about the delicious aroma of them baking made her mouth water.

Mattie was about to doze off when Mom entered her room. "Have you been in here all morning?" she asked.

Mattie shook her head. "I went sledding with Mark for a while, but it was too cold, so I came home, changed clothes, and crawled under my quilt to get warm."

"You look umgerennt," Mom said. "Is it because you had to quit sledding?"

Mattie shook her head. "That's not why I'm upset."

"What's the problem then?"

"I'm worried that you like Ada and Perry more than me."

Mom took a seat on the bed and held Mattie's hand. "What makes you think that?"

"You took Ada and Perry shopping today and didn't invite me to go along."

"That's because I didn't think you'd want to go. I figured it wouldn't be any fun for you to watch your little sister and brother try on new boots."

Mattie folded her arms. "It would have been better than staying here alone or falling off the sled into the cold snow and ending up all wet."

Mom gave Mattie a hug. "I can assure you that I love all my kinner the same."

Mattie smiled. "That's sure good to hear."

"Would you like to go with us this afternoon to Grandma Miller's house?" Mom asked.

"Jah, I would," Mattie replied. "I could keep Ada and Perry entertained while you and Grandma clean house."

"We'd appreciate that." Mom patted Mattie's arm. "Maybe next Saturday you and I can bake those pumpkin cookies. Would you like that?"

Mattie nodded eagerly.

"Come on then. Let's make some hot chocolate to warm you up. After that, if you like, you can help me clean Ada's room," Mom suggested. "That way we can leave sooner for your grandma and grandpa's house."

Mattie was all for that. She was glad to know Mom loved her as much as Ada and Perry. She could hardly wait until next Saturday to make pumpkin cookies!

CHAPTER 11

Rotten Bananas

The following Saturday morning, Mattie and Mom got ready to bake pumpkin cookies.

"I'll probably do some other baking today, too, but we'll do the cookies first," Mom said.

Mattie smiled. It was nice to spend time with Mom in the kitchen. She could almost taste the cookies that would soon be baking in their oven, not to mention the wonderful aroma that would linger long after they were baked. It would almost be like smelling those delicious pumpkin pies Mom had made for Thanksgiving.

"Would you please get out the ingredients we'll need for the kichlin?" Mom asked, handing Mattie a recipe card. "I'm going to the living room to see what Ada and Perry are up to, but I'll be back soon."

After Mom left the kitchen, Mattie began to set out the things they would need to make the cookies: flour, brown sugar, spices, raisins, nuts, vanilla, and cooking oil.

When Mattie went to the cupboard to get the flour, she spotted a bunch of bananas sitting on the counter.

They were ugly and black and felt soft and squishy.

"Eww. . ." Mattie wrinkled her nose. "These bananas are rotten." She scooped them up, marched across the room, and dropped them into the garbage can. "Good-bye, disgusting bananas!"

When Mom returned, she smiled at Mattie and said, "Did you get everything ready to start mixing the cookies?"

Mattie nodded and motioned to the kitchen table, where she'd placed all the ingredients.

"That's great," Mom said. "While you mix the batter, I'll get out the cookie sheets, and then I'm going to start mixing the ingredients for banana bread." Mom turned, and when she came to the place where the rotten bananas had been, she frowned. "What happened to the bananas? I know they were here a few minutes ago."

"I threw them out," Mattie said.

"Why did you do that?" Mom asked with a frown.

"They were rotten."

"They were just right for making banana bread. The inside of them was actually okay; just the outside peel looked bad," Mom explained. "You should have asked before you threw the bananas away."

"I'm sorry, Mom." Mattie swallowed hard. "I—I didn't know the bananas were still good."

"It's okay." Mom gave Mattie a hug. "Those banana peels did look pretty bad, and you had no way of knowing the bananas inside were just right for baking. We can still make pumpkin cookies, and I'll make banana bread some other time."

"Okay." Mattie felt a little better while she measured out the flour. "At least I learned something new about making banana bread."

"You're right, and that's a good way of looking at it," Mom agreed, stopping to glance out the window.

"I'll be glad when spring comes," Mattie said, following Mom's gaze at the falling snow as it built up on the outside windowsill. "Winter's cold, and the roads are *gfarlich*."

"Sometimes they can be dangerous," Mom agreed as she took the measuring spoons from the drawer. "However, it does no good to worry about it."

"Those were sure good pumpkin kichlin you and Mom baked on Saturday," Mark said as he and Mattie tromped through the snow on their way to school Monday morning. There was so much snow on the ground that the twins had decided to walk instead of ride their bike, as it would be hard to pedal in the deepening snow.

Mattie smiled. "I'm glad you liked 'em. Pumpkin's my favorite kind of kichlin. They smell so good when they're baking, too."

"I really like 'em, but my favorite kind of cookie is chocolate chip." Mark smacked his lips.

"*Brr*. . . It sure is cold out this morning," Mattie said,

talking through the scarf she'd wrapped around her nose and mouth, while pulling the collar of her jacket tightly around her neck.

"I know, and it's hard to walk in this schnee," Mark said, out of breath as he lifted each foot higher to take the next step. "We can't even shuffle through the snow because it's so deep. I'll be glad when it melts and we can ride our bike again."

Mattie nodded. "Same here, but at least it's not a blizzard. Not yet, anyway."

As they walked past the Bontragers' house, Mark noticed the pond on the right side of their place. "Did ya hear about Harley Bontrager?" he asked as they trudged through the deeper snow drifts that had piled up on this part of the road.

"No, I didn't. What about Harley?"

"When he was skating on his cousin's pond up in Wayne County, he fell through the ice."

Mattie gasped. "That's *baremlich*! Did he drown in that cold water?"

"You're right, it is terrible, but he's okay," Mark said. "His uncle was there when it happened, and he pulled Harley out of the water right away."

Mattie didn't say anything, but Mark could hear her breathing heavy as they plodded along. When they arrived at the schoolyard, Mattie turned to Mark and said, "I'm never goin' ice-skating again."

"How come?"

" 'Cause I'd be worried that I might fall through the ice." She shivered. "If nobody was there to rescue me, I'd probably drown. I can only imagine how cold that water must have been when Harley went through the ice. Makes me numb just thinkin' about it."

"You worry too much, Mattie. If you're careful about where you're skating and make sure the ice is good and thick, you'll be fine."

"Maybe so, but I'm never going ice-skating, so I don't have to worry about thin ice."

"Suit yourself," Mark said. "But if you never take a few chances in life, you'll miss out on a whole lot of fun."

"I don't care," Mattie responded. "All it takes is one mishap, and it can change everything."

"Well, I'm goin' ice-skating next Saturday evening with Ike. He's meetin' some of his friends and said he'd take me along. From what Ike told me, the pond we're goin' to is a really big one."

Mattie grasped the sleeve of Mark's jacket. "I don't think that's a good idea. Don't go, Mark. Please don't."

"Ike's our big brother, and I'm sure he wouldn't take me if it wasn't safe," Mark said. *My twin sister is nothing but a worrywart,* he thought. *But I wonder how bad it must have been when Harley fell through the ice.* Mark had once heard that it felt like a million needles when your skin came in contact with freezing water. He wasn't worried, however. Ike said he had been at this bigger pond before. It was located somewhere in the next county, and Ike's friend had told him that the skating was great there. Surely this pond would be monitored by whoever owned it. They would put up a sign if it wasn't safe for skating.

Mark kicked at the snow in front of him as they hurried to get inside the schoolhouse where it would be nice and warm. It'd be fun to go ice-skating, and Ike had mentioned that there would be a bonfire with hot dogs and marshmallows to roast. Mark was sure they would have a great time.

A Terrible Storm

"It's snowing really hard," Mattie said as she and Mark left the schoolhouse that afternoon. "I wish Calvin and Russell hadn't hurried ahead of us."

"Even if they'd walked with us, it wouldn't have changed the weather any," Mark said. "It would still be snowing as hard as it is now. Maybe if we hurry, we can walk in the path they made, and it'll be easier for us."

Mattie looked up at the giant snowflakes falling quickly from the sky and blinked as they stuck to her eyelashes. It was getting worse by the minute, and in no time, the wind had picked up speed. "I don't know, Mark. Our brothers' tracks are getting covered up really quick. I'm worried we might not make it home. Not only that, but my feet are so cold I can hardly walk." Mattie pulled her outer garment tightly around her, lowered her head, and leaned into the wind. The frigid air, which seemed to be trying its best to seep inside the warmth of her coat, was getting harder to ward off. The snow was no longer coming down in soft, wispy flakes like it had been earlier today. It was forced sideways by the wind and stung her cheeks and nose.

"We'll be okay. Just keep movin'," Mark said. "It will keep the blood circulating in our feet and help to keep 'em warm."

"You mean the blood is going around in circles inside our feet?" Mattie yelled above the howling wind.

"No, silly, it means the blood is flowing through the veins in our feet, and the circulation will help our feet not to freeze," Mark explained.

Just then, the old barn they went past every day came into view. It had been sitting empty for a long time, and no one used it anymore. The Smiths, who weren't Amish, had built a new barn several years ago, closer to their house, which sat way back from the road.

"Maybe we should go in there and wait till the weather gets better," Mattie said, pointing to the barn as she nearly stumbled. "It's getting hard to see where we're going, and I'll bet it's a lot warmer inside the barn than it is out here in this cold blizzard." Even though there were a few loose boards on the back side of the structure, the barn roof was still intact. A little protection would be better than none at all.

Mark shook his head. "Just keep moving, Mattie; you'll be fine."

She grabbed the sleeve of Mark's jacket and gave it a shake. "Please, let's stop. I'm really worried about the storm."

"Okay, Mattie, but only till the snow lets up a bit." Mark stopped walking and turned toward the barn.

Mattie followed in his footsteps, thankful he'd agreed to go inside.

When they entered the barn, a musty, damp smell caused Mattie to sneeze. "Ah-choo!"

"Bless you," said Mark as he and Mattie took a seat on a bale of straw. There was an old horse blanket there, too, and they huddled under that, trying to stay warm.

They sat quietly for several minutes, listening to the wind howl as it whipped the snow and swirled it around the outside of the barn. The force of the wind was so strong that snow could be seen seeping in through the back wall of the barn where the wood was falling apart.

Mattie turned to Mark and said, "I am *vergeksagdert*, aren't you?"

Mark shook his head. "There's nothing to be terrified of, Mattie. You're safe here with me. Besides, this old barn has been around a long time and held up through a lot of storms. I'm almost sure it won't come down now with us sittin' in it."

Mattie figured her twin brother was just trying to sound grown up. She could see by looking at his furrowed brows that he was worried, too. She blew on her left hand to keep it warm.

"Why don't ya put your other glove on?" Mark questioned.

"I think I lost it outside somewhere."

"Then you'd better put your hand under your coat to keep it warm," Mark said. "This is not a good time to be losin' your glove, sister."

Mattie groaned. "Don't remind me of that." She wished Twinkles were with her right now. Whenever she held the dog, she always felt relaxed.

Wo-o-o-sh! Wo-o-o-sh! The wind howled eerily from outside, rattling the windows and shaking the barn door. Pieces of straw floated down from the loft as the drafty air whisked through the upper level of the barn.

Mattie moved closer to Mark. As frightening as it was to be in this old barn, she'd be more afraid if she were outside right now. If not for this shelter, they might have gotten buried in the snow trying to get home. She'd heard stories about people getting lost just going from their house to the barn in blizzards such as this. The storm didn't sound like it would be letting up anytime soon, either, so Mattie was glad she and Mark weren't out there in the blinding snow.

"What can we do while we're waiting for the storm to pass?" Mattie asked her brother.

He shrugged. "I don't know. Guess we could play a game."

Mattie's forehead wrinkled. "What kind of game? There are no games in here, Mark."

"We can play a question-and-answer game," he said. "I'll ask some questions, and you can answer them."

"What kind of questions?" Mattie wanted to know.

Mark tapped his chin a couple of times. "Let's see now. . . . Guess I'll just ask you whatever pops into my mind."

Mattie sighed. "I suppose that would be okay—as long as you don't use any big words."

He frowned. "It won't be any fun if I can't use big words."

Mattie folded her arms. "Guess I won't play the game then."

"Oh, all right." Mark tapped his chin a couple more times. "Okay, here's the first question. What's the best way to attract a hummingbird?"

"Now what kind of a question is that?" Mattie asked. "It's the middle of winter, and there are no hummingbirds here this time of the year."

"I know that, but they come every summer, and it's fun to watch 'em eat at the feeders Mom always puts out."

"That's true."

"So what's the best way to attract the hummers?" Mark asked.

"By putting out our feeders," Mattie replied.

Mark shook his head. "I meant without the feeders."

Mattie shrugged. "I don't know."

"You can attract them by plantin' flowers in the yard, such as honeysuckle, butterfly bush, trumpet vine, fuchsia, and—"

"Snapdragons," Mattie interrupted. "Some of the hummingbirds that have come into our yard get nectar from the snapdragons Mom has planted near the house."

Mark smiled. "See, you do know about the flowers that will attract hummingbirds. I thought you would, since you like wildflowers so well."

"That's right," Mattie said with a nod. "And the hummers especially like the color red. That's why most hummingbird feeders have a red base." She glanced toward the barn door, already tired of the little game Mark had thought up. "I wonder if the schnee is letting up. It's cold in here, and I'd like to go home."

Mark stood and went over to the door, but when he tried to open it, nothing happened.

"What's wrong?" Mattie asked, jumping up from her seat and rushing to the door.

"It won't open." Mark's blue eyes widened. "I—I think we're trapped."

Mattie grasped the door handle and pushed on the door, but it didn't budge.

"Maybe the snow's coming down so hard that it's piled up by the door. There could be a big drift pushing against it, and that might be the reason we can't get it to open."

Mattie gulped. "Oh no! We might be stuck in here forever."

"Don't be so melodramatic," Mark said.

She scrunched up her nose and stared at him. "I'm not *melodramatic*. I'm *worried*."

"Maybe if we go to the back of the barn where the

boards are loose, we can pull some of 'em aside enough so we can try and squeeze through," Mark said.

"Jah, let's see if we can." Mattie jumped up, grateful that they had another option. "I hope it will work."

The twins worked their way toward the rear of the barn, crawling over more bales of straw and then over a pile of old lumber. It was a bit difficult in the now-darkened barn, but somehow they managed to find their way through all the obstacles. Their eyes had adjusted to the dimness inside, and when they reached the back section, they stood and surveyed the few wobbly pieces of boards that were hanging by only a nail or two.

"I think if we try to get those two boards loose, it'll give us enough room to squeeze through to the outside," Mark said. "Let's see if we can work the boards apart enough to pull 'em off the wall."

"Okay, but we'd better be careful of those nails sticking out." Mattie pointed to one end of the plank. "The nails are old, just like this barn, and I'll bet they're rusty. We don't wanna get punctured by one of them. We could get a bad infection if that happened."

"Since I have both of my gloves, you'd better let me try to work the boards free," Mark said, sounding confident. "I'm sure you're right. Those nails are probably corroded."

"Corroded? What does that mean?"

"It means rusty, just like you said. Or it could also mean decayed or eaten away," Mark explained as he yanked on the first board. Thankfully, that one came right off the wall, and he heaved it to one side.

Before Mark reached for the second board, which Mattie hoped would allow enough space for them to squeeze through, he peered through the opening where the other loose board had been. "Don't think it's gonna work, Mattie," Mark said with a shake of his head.

"How come? Just one more board and we'll be able to get out of here and head for home." Mattie was tired of being in the old chilly barn.

"We can't do it, unless you wanna be swallowed up by a whole bunch of snow." Mark groaned. "There's a snowdrift on this end of the barn, too. If we go through where the opening is, we'll be jumping right into it. How would anybody find us then?"

"Oh Mark, you're right; we sure can't do that. But then how will anyone find us in here? Now I'm really worried," Mattie whined as they made their way back to the front of the barn.

"Well, you shouldn't be worried. I'm sure once Mom realizes we're not home on time, she'll send Dad or one of our brothers to come looking for us." Mark motioned to the bale of straw where they'd been sitting before. "Since this building is on the way home from school, I'm sure they'll think to look here when they go out searching for us."

"Let's hope you're right," Mattie quietly answered.

"While we're waitin' for help to arrive, let's play

another question-and-answer game," Mark suggested.

"I don't want to," Mattie said. "I'm too naerfich to answer any more of your questions."

"You don't have to be nervous," Mark said, taking a seat beside her. "Let's pray and ask God to help us."

"You're right; we should do that," Mattie agreed. Sitting on the bale of straw, she bowed her head. "Dear Jesus," she prayed out loud, "please send someone to rescue us, and help me to trust You and not worry so much."

"Let's sing one of the songs we've learned at school," Mark suggested after Mattie's prayer ended. "It'll help us relax and take our mind off the predicament we're in."

"Pre-dic-a-*what*?"

"Predicament. It's the same as saying we're in a mess, a fix, or a bind."

Mattie bobbed her head. "Jah, we're in a big mess all right. I should never have suggested we come into this old barn. We should have kept walking toward home, no matter how hard the snow was coming down."

Mark reached for Mattie's gloved hand. "Let's sing the 'Little Children' song."

"Okay," Mattie squeaked. That song seemed to fit their situation, since she felt like a little child right now.

"Sing, little children, sing, sing," Mark and Mattie sang at the top of their lungs. "God is good, and He cares for you. Sing, little children, sing."

Mattie started the second verse, and Mark sang, too.

"Pray, little children, pray, pray. God is good, and He cares for you. Pray, little children, pray."

"Wish I'd never listened to you and come in here," Mark said to Mattie sometime later as they huddled under the horse blanket together. "If we'd kept going, we'd be home by now, sitting in Mom's kitchen with a cup of hot chocolate and some of those pumpkin kichlin you and Mom made."

Mattie sniffed as tears rolled down her cheeks. She was cold and frightened, and now she felt guilty. "I–I'm sorry," she murmured. "I wish we'd gone home, too. I was worried we might lose our way when we couldn't see, and then we'd have really been in a *predicament*."

"Now don't start cryin', Mattie. It's making me feel sad." Mark tickled Mattie under her chin. "Does that make you feel any better?"

She pushed his hand aside. "No, and I don't want to be tickled right now."

"Sorry. I just thought it might make you feel better."

"I'll feel better when somebody comes and rescues us," Mattie replied.

"I agree." Mark glanced at Mattie's lunch pail sitting at her feet. "Do you have any more of those pumpkin kichlin, or did ya eat all of 'em at lunch?"

"Sorry, Mark. I ate them all. What about the ones Mom put in your lunch box?"

Mark shook his head. "I ate all of mine, too." His stomach rumbled noisily.

Mattie giggled. Mark laughed, too.

"I wonder if Mom and Dad will be mad at us." Mark's expression and tone of voice had turned serious.

"I wonder if we'll have to spend the night in this old barn." Mattie shivered and moved a little closer to Mark. Then she tipped her head to one side. "Did you hear that?"

"Hear what?" he asked.

"Listen, there it is again."

Whoo-hoot! Whoo-hoot! Whoo-hoot!

"I hear it now." Mark pointed to the rafters. "I think there's an owl up there."

Mattie tilted her head way back and stared up above. "I don't see anything. 'Course, it's really dim in here—especially up there in the rafters."

"Sure wish we had a flashlight," Mark said. "Pretty soon we won't be able to see anything at all. Maybe our eyes will adjust as it gets darker."

"Do you think we'll freeze to death if help doesn't come soon?" Mattie's chin quivered, just thinking about it.

Mark patted her arm. "Naw, we'll be okay. Just close your eyes and keep praying. Someone's bound to come lookin' for us."

Mattie closed her eyes and leaned her head on Mark's shoulder. She felt kind of drowsy all of a sudden. Maybe if she slept awhile it would make the time go quicker. She could tell by Mark's steady breathing that he was getting sleepy, too.

Mattie thought about a Bible verse Dad had read to them once, Psalm 56:3: "When I am afraid, I will put my trust in you." That helped her feel a bit better, and she took a deep breath, trying to relax.

Suddenly, the barn door rattled, and then Mattie heard voices.

"Mark! Mattie! Are you in there?"

Her eyes snapped open, and so did Mark's. "We're here! We're here!" they yelled at the same time. Help had finally come. God had answered their prayers. They were about to be rescued!

"We were worried about you two," Mom said, looking at Mark and Mattie from across the supper table that evening.

"That's right," Dad said with a nod. "When you didn't come home right away after school, we thought at first that the teacher might have kept you there because of the storm."

"But Anna Ruth didn't keep Russell and me," Calvin said, reaching for the salt and adding some to the green beans on his plate. "So we told Dad that we didn't think she'd kept you two, either."

"How long were you looking for us?" Mark questioned.

"We didn't start right away," Dad explained. "We waited awhile, hoping you'd show up, but when it started getting dark, and you still weren't home, we became concerned." He took a drink of water. "So I hitched my horse to the buggy, and Ike and I headed straight for the schoolhouse."

"That's right," Ike agreed. "But when we got there and saw that everyone, including Anna Ruth, was gone, we really got worried."

Mark looked over at Mattie and said, "I guess even grown-ups and teenagers worry sometimes."

"That's true," Mom put in, "but I try not to worry about every little thing." Her forehead wrinkled. "However, something like missing children is enough to make any parent worry."

"How'd you know to look for us in that old barn?" Mattie asked. "Did you see our footsteps in the snow and follow them there?"

Dad shook his head. "The snow was too deep to see any footsteps. However, when we found one of Mattie's gloves stuck to a bush near the barn, we had a hunch you two may have taken shelter inside."

"Remember, Mattie? I gave you the missing glove that we found, and you said how cold your one hand was," Ike reminded her.

"Oh, that's right. Maybe there was a reason I lost that glove. Maybe it was to help you find us."

"You both made the right choice by going in the barn

and taking shelter from the storm," Mom added.

"That's what we did, all right," Mark said. "We thought we could wait there till the snow let up, but it got worse, not better. *Mir hen bang ghat.*"

"That's right," Mattie agreed. "We were afraid."

"When we tried to push open the barn door, it was stuck." Mattie wiped her mouth on a napkin. "I was really scared at first, but then we prayed and that made me feel a little better."

"It's always good to pray when we're in a difficult situation," Mom said. "When your daed and Ike were out looking for you, I was here praying, too."

"God answered our prayers, and I'm glad we're home where it's warm and we can eat. Sure wouldn't have wanted to miss supper." Mark's stomach growled, and everyone laughed. He didn't care; he was just happy to be safe and at home with his family.

CHAPTER 13

Thin Ice

It was the perfect evening to go ice-skating, and Mark was really excited. After the heavy snowfall they'd had earlier in the week, the skies had cleared, and today had been bright with sunshine. Now, after the western horizon had glowed orange and pink, a few stars became visible as the night sky began to turn black. Someone had brought several torches, which they'd stuck in the snow around the pond. That helped to light things up well enough so they could all see. Some of the kids also had flashlights and battery-operated lanterns.

As Mark sat on a tree stump and laced up his skates, he watched some of the other boys already gliding on the ice. There was still a light covering of snow on top of the ice, but he could see where most of it had been shoveled off to one side.

"What do you think of this pond?" Ike asked as he stood and waited for Mark to finish with his skates.

"It's a lot bigger than I expected." Mark was really impressed, especially since the ponds around their home were so much smaller.

"I don't get to come up here very often, but whenever my friend Wayne invites me, I try not to pass up the opportunity," Ike said. "Wayne said this is a popular ice-skating spot, and from the looks of all the kids that are here, I think he's right about that."

Mark smiled up at Ike, feeling pleased that they could do something fun together. Since Ike had started courting his girlfriend, Catherine, several months ago, Mark didn't get to spend much time with his big brother. "I'm glad you invited me to come along. Mom and Dad said if I got all my chores done today, I could go, so I hurried up and got 'em finished right away."

"Let's do some skating now," Ike said as he stepped onto the frozen pond. "Our driver said he'd be back for us in two or three hours, so we don't want to waste any time."

Mark joined his brother and the others. Around and around the pond they went. This was great! Even with the other boys and girls skating on the pond, there was still plenty of room, and nobody seemed to get in anyone's way.

"I'll bet this *deich* is bigger than a skating rink," Mark called to Ike as they chased each other around.

"You could be right about that," Ike said with a wink. "It's a very large pond."

Mark noticed there weren't many houses nearby, so he didn't know who owned the pond. He also saw that at one end of the pond there was a huge stack of firewood, where smoke billowed slowly up as one of the boys lit a bonfire.

Mark was having fun making figure eights. It had taken a lot of practice, but last year he'd taught himself to skate backward, too. Tonight, as he glided back and forth across the ice, he was glad he hadn't forgotten how to skate backward or make figure eights.

"I hope Mark and Ike will be safe on the ice this evening," Mattie said as she and Mom did the supper dishes. "I'm worried about them."

"Try not to worry so much," Mom said, sloshing her sponge over one of the plates. "Ike has skated on that pond before, and I'm sure he will watch out for thin ice and make sure he and Mark don't skate anyplace where it might be dangerous."

"How come Russell and Calvin didn't go skating with them?" Mattie asked as she reached for a clean dish to dry.

"I believe Ike invited them, but they said it was too cold, and that they'd rather stay home and work on a puzzle they had started the other day." Mom drained the water from the sink. "That's the last of the dishes now. As soon as you've finished drying them, you can do whatever you like."

"Maybe I'll go up to my room and make a few bookmarks with some of my dried flowers," Mattie said.

Mom smiled. "That's a good idea. It'll keep your

mind and hands busy, so you won't have time to worry about Mark and Ike. Oh, and you should say a prayer for them, too," she added.

After about an hour of skating with Mark, Ike joined some of the older boys who were getting a game of "crack the whip" started. All the players got in a line, each holding hands with the person in front of them, as well as the person in back. As they skated together, the person at the front of the line suddenly veered off in another direction, making everyone else whip quickly around. It looked like a fun game—especially for those at the tail end of the chain. They were lucky if they could hang on.

As Mark skated toward the other end of the pond, away from those playing the game, he thought he heard a noise. *What was that?* he wondered as he stopped to listen. But all he could hear was the laughter of the boys, who were obviously having a good time. Mark figured it was just his imagination. For some reason, though, Mattie's warning to be careful tonight kept creeping into his brain.

Mark paused a minute and heard the noise again. This time the sound was very distinctive, and he knew right away what it was. *Click! Click! Snap! Crackle!*

Skating quickly over to the group playing the game, Mark motioned to Ike.

"You should come join us!" Ike called. "Being whipped around is a lot of fun, especially if you're the one at the very end."

Mark shook his head and skated closer to his brother, being careful to watch for any areas of thin ice. "Did anyone check this deich to make sure it's safe?" he asked. "I don't see any houses real close, and I wonder if anyone owns the pond."

Just then, Ike's friend Wayne skated up to them. "Come on, Ike. You're holding up the game. What are ya doin' anyways?"

"I was asking my bruder if someone checks this pond to make sure it's safe for people to skate on," Mark said before Ike could answer his friend. He pointed to the left. "I was skatin' over there and heard some cracking sounds. I think we should get off the ice before someone falls through."

"You fellows aren't scared, are ya?" one of the other boys, whose name was Melvin, asked, joining the threesome.

Mark put his hands on his hips and stared up at the boy. "I just wanna make sure the deich is safe for all of us to be on."

"It's perfectly safe, and I think you're a chicken." Melvin squinted his pale blue eyes as he looked at Ike. "Maybe you should have left your little bruder at home this evening. We don't want him scaring everyone and makin' them leave the pond because he thought heard a noise."

"Chicken or not, I agree with my brother," Ike stated, placing his hands on his hips. "Come on, Mark. Let's get off the ice and go check on the fire to see if it's ready for some roasting."

Wayne joined Mark and Ike as they made their way over to the bonfire. Shortly after, a few more boys did the same, mumbling that they were hungry. Melvin, along with some of his friends, didn't seem to care about eating, and they started a game of hockey.

"I'm really not a chicken," Mark said, "but when I heard the ice crackin', it made me naerfich."

Ike squeezed Mark's shoulder. "It's okay. I understand. Besides, it's definitely time for us to get something to eat."

Another boy, whom Mark had never met before, joined the conversation as Mark and Ike started to remove their skates. "Don't worry," he said while putting a hot dog on the end of a stick. "I heard the cracking noise, too, but you spoke up before I got the chance."

Mark felt better hearing that. There were several more boys around the bonfire now, too.

As they all stood closer to the flames, letting its warmth take away the chill, Mark couldn't help glancing toward the pond where those other boys still skated. A shiver went through him as the night air suddenly felt colder. Was it because he had stopped skating and wasn't as warm, or was it something else that made him tremble?

"I'm hungerich." Ike smacked his lips and grabbed a hot dog. "It's more comfortable here by the fire than it is out there on the ice—especially now that I'm cooling off. I worked up a good sweat when we were playing crack the whip, but I think I worked up an even better appetite."

"But what about the cracking ice I heard?" Mark asked.

"Well, if there is any thin ice, then it's safer for us here," Ike said.

Mark nodded, and then relaxing a little, he held his hot dog over the coals, eagerly waiting for it to get done so he could eat. "Danki for inviting me along tonight, Ike. I've had a great time."

Ike grinned and gave Mark's shoulder a tap. "I'm glad, little brother. It's been fun to be with you."

After the hot dogs were roasted, they all made their way to an old log that was now being used for a seat. The hot dogs, chips, and pretzels were hurriedly eaten, and most of the boys had hot chocolate, too. Mark thought food always tasted better when it was eaten outside—especially after some vigorous exercise like ice-skating.

"Think I'm ready to roast some marshmallows now," Wayne said, rising from his seat.

"We'll join you in a few minutes," Ike replied, eating the last of his chips.

Then, all of a sudden, at the far end of the pond, someone yelled, "Help! The ice broke! Help! Help!"

Mark looked at Ike, and Ike looked at Mark. Then everyone who'd been sitting on the log ran quickly around the edge of the pond toward the pleas for help. When they reached the other side, a few of the boys stood pointing at a spot not far from the end of the pond. There, hanging on to the edge of the broken ice, was Melvin, who had previously made fun of Mark. The bottom half of his body was submerged in the frigid, numbing water. "Help me," said the whimpering boy, who'd earlier seemed so sure of himself.

While everyone stood with their mouths hanging open, Ike looked around. Not far from them were some hockey sticks, and he quickly grabbed hold of one. "Hang on!" Ike called to the struggling boy. "We'll get you out!"

Ike turned to the others and said, "Let's make a human chain. One of us needs to slide out to Melvin on their belly, and then someone can hang on to their feet. Oh, and if anyone has a cell phone, you'd better call for help."

"I should go out to help Melvin," Mark spoke up. "I'm the smallest, so I'll have a better chance of not fallin' through the ice."

"No way!" Ike shook his head forcibly, taking charge of the situation. "I'm not taking the chance of you falling in, too."

"Let him do it," one of the other boys said. "We'll hang on to him and to each other. We will make sure he's safe."

"Please, Ike, let me do it," Mark pleaded. He was scared, but at the same time, he really wanted to help rescue Melvin.

"Okay," Ike finally said. "But whatever you do, once Melvin's holding the end of the hockey stick, don't let go."

"I—I won't." Mark could see that his brother was afraid for him, but this was something he felt he must do.

With his heart hammering in his chest, Mark lay down and slowly bellied his way across the ice while each of the boys held on to the other's feet. Mark kept the hockey stick out in front of him, never taking his eyes off Melvin. "Hang on tight to my feet," he called to Ike. "I'm almost there. So far, so good."

"Don't worry. I've got ya," Ike said in an encouraging tone.

In no time, Mark was a few feet from the gaping hole where Melvin held on to the edge of the ice. Stretching the hockey stick as far as he could, Mark told Melvin to grab for it.

"I—I'm afraid to let go." Melvin's voice shook, and his brown eyes were wide with fear.

Mark said a silent prayer: *Dear Jesus, please help us get Melvin out of the freezing water.*

"You can do it!" Ike hollered. "Just reach for the stick, and we'll pull you out."

It seemed that was all the poor fellow needed, for Melvin thrust forward and grabbed the end of the hockey stick.

"I've got him! Now everyone pull with all your might!"

Mark hollered as he felt his brother's grip tighten even more around his ankles.

Without breaking any more ice, the human chain managed to pull Melvin out of the water just as a siren could be heard in the distance. Thankfully, someone owned a cell phone and had called for help.

Ike wrapped a blanket around the shivering boy while someone else handed him a steaming cup of hot chocolate to help keep him warm until the ambulance arrived.

"Danki," Melvin said, looking at everyone who had helped. Then he looked right at Mark, and through chattering teeth he said, "You were br–brave to do what you did, and I–I'm s–sorry for making f–fun of you before. Y–you may be smaller than me, but you're a whole lot w–wiser."

Mark smiled, although his heart was beating so hard he could feel it pounding in his chest. "It's okay. I'm just glad you're safe."

As the rescue vehicle pulled in, Mark picked up his skates while the others doused the fire. "I don't know about you," he said to Ike, "but I'm tired of winter."

Ike nodded. "Jah, me, too, but winter's not so bad if you're careful and try to be safe."

Mattie was right to be worried about thin ice on the pond, Mark thought. *From now on, I'll be very careful whenever I skate.*

CHAPTER 14

A Valuable Lesson

By the first week of March, the snow was all gone, and Mattie looked forward to spring so she could be outside in her little garden. She was eager to see the flowers bloom and watch the birds build nests in the trees. She was even looking forward to watching for Mark's frog when it emerged from hibernation. The only thing Mattie didn't like about spring was all the rain they usually got. Yesterday was one of those days. It had begun raining the previous night and hadn't stopped until early that morning.

Mattie stared out her bedroom window and noticed Mom hanging clothes on the line. It was a good thing it had stopped raining, or she would have been hanging them in the basement instead of outside. Even so, Mattie could see there were still some droplets of water falling from the line each time Mom hung up an item.

This was Saturday, and since Mattie didn't have school, she was looking forward to getting outside. The grass would still be wet, but it didn't matter. It was better than trying to maneuver in the deep snow they'd had over the winter months.

Maybe I'll spend some time with Twinkles today, Mattie thought. *We could play fetch with the new ball she got for Christmas.*

Tap! Tap! Tap!

Mattie turned away from the window. "Come in!" she called.

The door opened, and Mark stepped into her room. "I need to talk to you," he said with a worried expression.

"What about?"

"Mom and Dad." Mark's voice lowered to a whisper as he moved closer to Mattie. "They're going broke."

Mattie's mouth opened wide. "How do you know?"

"I heard 'em talkin' about it awhile ago—before Mom went outside to hang up the clothes." Mark frowned. "I'm really worried, Mattie. What's gonna happen if Mom and Dad don't have enough money to take care of us anymore?"

Mattie's eyes widened. "Are you sure about this, Mark? What exactly did you hear them say?"

"Mom asked if Dad could buy a bigger buggy for us all to ride in, but Dad said he couldn't afford it right now and that business was slow in the wood shop."

"Buggies are expensive," Mattie said. "Just 'cause Dad said he can't buy a new buggy doesn't mean our folks are going broke."

"That wasn't all I heard," Mark shook his head.

"Mom said she was gonna grow some more vegetables in her garden this summer so she wouldn't have to spend as much money on groceries. She also mentioned tryin' to sell some of the things she's sewn over the winter to bring in extra money."

Mattie turned and stared out the window again, watching as Mom hung on the line the beautiful quilt that she kept on her and Dad's bed. If her folks didn't have enough money to take care of their family, Mattie wondered what they would do. Now she had something else to worry about, and she knew that Mark must be worried, too.

"My everyday shoes are getting a little bit tight," she said. "Guess I'd better not say anything to Mom about that, though. At least not till she and Dad are makin' more money."

"I need to run a few errands today," Mom told the twins after they'd finished their lunch that afternoon. "I'll be taking Ada and Perry over to your grandpa and grandma Miller's on my way into town and leaving them while I shop. Would you two like to go along?"

Mark looked at Mattie, and Mattie looked at Mark. "I'd rather stay here with Twinkles," Mattie said.

"I'll stay, too," Mark added. "Think I might play with my katze, or maybe if it's windy enough, I'll try flyin' my kite."

"We should play some ball," Mattie said. She bumped

her brother's arm. "You need the practice, right?"

"We'll see," Mark mumbled.

"If you don't want to play ball with me, then maybe I'll plant some seeds in my little garden," Mattie said. "I'll scatter them between our two garden plaques."

"Oh, I almost forgot. . . I need to put the little frog pool out there, too, Mark said excitedly. Think I'd better do that right away, before you start plantin' your seeds."

Mom smiled and gave the twins a little pat on the head. "That's fine; you can do whatever you like. You two worked hard getting your chores done this morning, so now you deserve to have some fun. I shouldn't be gone too long, but if you get hungry, feel free to fix a snack. Calvin and Russell are going to visit one of their friends, but your daed and Ike are out in the shop, so if you need anything just let them know."

"Okay," said Mattie, "but I'm sure we'll be fine. We're not babies anymore."

Mom smiled and patted the top of Mattie's head. "I know you're not, daughter." She turned toward the house.

Mark smiled. He hoped playing with Boots and Lucky for a while would help him not to worry so much about his folks' finances. He wished there was something he could do to help out.

A short time later, Mark was outside blowing bubbles while his two cats zipped around the yard, chasing after them. Mattie was in the barn, playing with Twinkles. It was a good thing, too, because if the dog had been out here, she probably would have been chasing after the cats.

Mark had only been blowing bubbles a short time when Mattie came out of the barn with Twinkles.

Oh great, he thought. *Now my fun is over. That hund of Mattie's will probably start chasin' my katze.*

"I thought we were gonna play ball," Mattie said, joining Mark on the lawn.

He shook his head. "I never said that. . .just said I'd see."

"Don't you want to get better at playing baseball?" she asked.

He shrugged. "Don't see why I need to. I'm not that fond of the game."

"I'm not that fond of spelling, either, but I still try to get a good grade."

"That's different. It's important to do well in school. Baseball isn't required for us to graduate when we get to the eighth grade," Mark said. "Besides, I'm busy right now, blowin' bubbles."

"Can I blow some?" Mattie asked.

"Jah, sure." Mark handed the jar of bubbles to Mattie, and they both knelt on the grass near the clothesline. It was still damp from the rain, but Mark didn't mind. Only his knees would get wet.

"We should get the bubble maker Grandpa Miller

gave us for Christmas." Mattie grinned. "I'd like to see my hund and your katze go after those big bubbles."

"I wanted to use up the liquid in this bottle first. Then we can get the homemade one and make gigantic bubbles," Mark explained.

They took turns blowing bubbles while Twinkles, Lucky, and Boots raced back and forth, leaping into the air to try and catch the bubbles. At least Twinkles wasn't chasing the cats. For now, she seemed more interested in the bubbles.

"Be careful you don't blow any bubbles near Mom's *gwilde*," Mattie warned.

"The bubbles won't hurt the quilt," Mark said. "Besides, most of 'em are gettin' popped before they rise very high."

"I wish our bubbles could reach all the way up to heaven," Mattie said after she'd blown another bubble.

"I know, but they can't, 'cause they would pop." Mark grabbed the bubble wand and blew a giant bubble that floated above Mattie's head. He reached up and popped it. "See what I mean?"

"Absatz!" Mattie poked Mark's arm. "You're always teasing."

He grinned. "I know, but you like it sometimes."

When the twins got tired of blowing bubbles, they took a walk over to Mattie's garden, and Mark set the frog pool in place. "No sign of the *frosch* yet," Mark said, bending down to look in the opening of his frog house.

"Don't worry," said Mattie. "I'm sure he'll come out of hibernation soon. He's probably burrowed in the dirt underneath the frog house."

"Well, since we can't watch the frosch and there are no birds drinkin' from the little pool yet, why don't we get our kites and try to fly 'em?" Mark suggested. "The wind's picked up a bit, so it's perfect weather for kites."

"Sure, that sounds like fun."

Mattie and Mark were about to head for the house to get their kites when a small blue car pulled into the yard. Then a middle-aged woman with short brown hair got out and walked over to them. "Can you tell me where the Walnut Creek Cheese Store is?" she asked.

"It's that way." Mark pointed to the road that ran along the right side of their property.

The woman smiled, and then looking toward the clothesline, she said, "That's a beautiful quilt. Is it for sale?"

"No," said Mattie. "It belongs to our mom."

"Oh, that's too bad," the woman said. "I'd be willing to pay a fair price for it."

Mattie shook her head, but Mark stepped up to the lady and asked, "How much would you pay for it?"

"I've seen some other quilts similar to this, and they were selling for $800, so I'd be willing to pay that much. I'd have to speak to your mother first, of course," the woman added.

"Our mother isn't home at the moment," Mark

stated. "But our folks need money right now, and Mom's gonna try to sell some things. So I'm sure she'd be real pleased if you bought the quilt."

The woman nodded. "Why, thank you. I think I will."

"I don't think selling Mom's gwilde is a good idea," Mattie whispered in Mark's ear.

Ignoring his sister's comment, Mark took the lady's money, smiled, and said, "Thank you." He could hardly wait until Mom got home so he could give her the money. But looking over at his sister and seeing the worried expression on her face, Mark wondered, *Did I do the right thing?*

"Mom's gonna be upset when she finds out what you did," Mattie said after the woman left with the quilt.

Mark shook his head. "No, she won't. She and Dad need the money, and since Mom said she was gonna try to sell a few things she's made, I'm sure she'll be glad I sold her gwilde."

Mattie wasn't sure about that, but maybe her brother was right. Eight hundred dollars was a lot of money that would surely help their parents out. She hoped so anyway.

When the twins got tired of blowing bubbles, they went into the house to get a snack.

"I wonder how long Mom will be gone," Mattie said as she took a jar of peanut butter down from the kitchen cupboard. "Did she say where she was going?"

Mark shrugged his shoulders. "I have no idea."

"What kind of crackers do you want—multigrain or the whole-wheat kind?" Mattie asked.

Mark tapped his chin a couple of times. "Hmm. . . I can't decide."

"Okay, I have an idea," Mattie said. "Close your eyes, and I'll give you two different crackers to taste. Then you can decide which one you like best."

Mark nodded eagerly. "That sounds like a good idea." He leaned against the counter, closed his eyes, and opened his mouth. "Okay, I'm ready."

Mattie giggled as she popped the first cracker into Mark's mouth. He chewed it up and smacked his lips. "All right, I'm ready for the next one."

Mattie put the second cracker in Mark's mouth, and he chewed that one up, too. "Yum. They're both good. It's hard to differentiate."

"Differ-*what*?"

"Differentiate. It means it's hard to tell 'em apart, so I'll take some of both." Mark opened his eyes.

"I figured you might."

After Mattie set out some peanut butter, crackers, and an apple for each of them, she and Mark took a seat at the table. As they ate their snack, they talked about their parents' financial situation.

"Sure wish I was done with school and could get a job to help out," Mark said.

"Well, you're not, so we just need to pray that Dad gets more work in the wood shop."

"I know. It's hard not to worry, though, isn't it?" Mattie nodded.

Mark tipped his head as he heard the *clip-clop* of a horse's hooves coming up the driveway. "Sounds like Mom is home," he said, rising from his seat and going to look out the kitchen window. Sure enough, Mom had pulled her horse up to the hitching rail, and she was helping Ada and Perry out of the buggy.

Mark drew in a deep breath. *I hope Mom's okay with me selling her quilt.*

Several minutes later, Mom and the little ones entered the house. When they stepped into the kitchen, Mom smiled at Mattie and said, "Did you take some of the things off the clothesline? I noticed that my quilt wasn't there."

Mattie looked at Mark, and Mark stared at the floor. "Uh, Mom, I have to tell you something," he mumbled

"What's that?" she asked.

"I sold your gwilde today." He looked up at her with a feeling of dread.

Mom's eyebrows shot up. "You sold my beautiful quilt the one your daed and I keep on our bed?"

"Jah."

"Oh Mark, why would you do such a thing?"

"I heard you and Dad talking about your finances this morning, and. . ."

"You were listening in on our conversation?" Deep lines formed across Mom's forehead. She looked really upset. Mom paused and sent Ada and Perry out of the room. "You know better than to do something like that," she said, shaking her finger at Mark. "Listening to other people's conversation without them knowing is called *eavesdropping*, and it's wrong."

"Sorry, Mom, but I wasn't listening on purpose. I just happened to hear what you said. When Dad mentioned that he didn't have enough money to buy a new buggy, and you said. . ." Mark stopped talking and swallowed around the lump in his throat. "You said you might try to sell some of the items you'd sewn this winter." He looked up at Mom with tears in his eyes. "Since you're out of money, I wanted to help, and when a lady came into the yard today and wanted to buy the quilt, I said yes." He pointed to the money lying on the counter.

Mom sank into a chair at the table and buried her face in her hands. "That was one of my favorite quilts," she sobbed. "My friend Vera gave it to me when your daed and I got married. And for your information, we are not out of money. Things are a little tight right now, but we'll manage just fine."

Mark felt terrible about what he'd done, and he apologized to Mom again. "I wish I could get your gwilde back, but I don't know who that lady is or where she lives."

"Until today we'd never seen her before," Mattie spoke up.

"Were you in on this, too, Mattie?" Mom asked.

"No. Well, jah, in a way I was," Mattie admitted. "I told Mark I didn't think it was a good idea, but I should have said more before it was too late."

Mom sighed deeply. "Well, what's done is done. Crying about it won't bring back my quilt." She looked at Mark and Mattie with a stern expression. "I hope you two have learned something from this today. You need to think before you act, because some actions can't be turned around or taken back. All of this came about from you worrying so much."

The twins both nodded soberly. Mark figured they would surely be punished.

Just then, a knock sounded on the back door. "I'll get it," Mattie said, hurrying from the room.

When Mattie returned to the kitchen a few minutes later, Mark was surprised to see that the woman he'd sold the quilt to was with her. She held Mom's quilt in her hands.

"I didn't feel right about buying this without your mother's permission," the woman said, looking at Mark. "So I decided to come back and talk to her first."

Mom stepped forward with a look of relief. "I'm so glad you did. My son shouldn't have sold you the quilt, and I'd really like it back. You see, the quilt is very special to me." She picked up the money Mark had placed on the counter and was about to hand it to the woman, when she paused and said, "Say, I have an idea."

"What's that?" the woman asked.

"How about I make you a quilt similar to this one?"

The woman smiled. "Yes, I would like that."

"Let's go into my sewing room, and I'll show you some material," Mom said. "That way you can pick out the colors you'd like."

"That would be wonderful." The woman handed Mom the quilt and followed her out of the kitchen.

Mark leaned against the counter and blew out his breath. "I'm glad that all worked out."

"Me, too," Mattie said. "You know, I've been thinking. . . If worry is like a bubble, and it will soon blow away, maybe we shouldn't worry so much. Maybe whenever we start to worry about something, we should blow some bubbles and let all our troubles go up in the air. You know, let the bubbles carry our troubles away."

Mark smiled. "Bubble troubles, right?"

Mattie gave a happy nod.

Mattie's Pumpkin Cookies

Ingredients:
1 cup brown sugar
1 cup cooked pumpkin
2 cups cooking oil
1 teaspoon vanilla
2 cups sifted flour
1 teaspoon baking soda
1 teaspoon baking powder
½ teaspoon salt
½ teaspoon cinnamon
½ teaspoon nutmeg
¼ teaspoon ginger
1 cup raisins
½ cup chopped nuts

In large mixing bowl beat together brown sugar, pumpkin, cooking oil, and vanilla. In separate bowl, sift together dry ingredients, then add to other ingredients and stir until smooth. Blend in raisins and nuts. Drop by spoonfuls onto greased baking sheet. Bake at 350 degrees for 12 to 15 minutes. Makes 3 to 4 dozen. Cookies will be soft and moist.

About the Author

WANDA E. BRUNSTETTER is a bestselling author who enjoys writing historical, as well as Amish-themed novels. Descended from Anabaptists herself, Wanda became fascinated with the Plain People when she married her husband, Richard, who grew up in a Mennonite church in Pennsylvania. Wanda and her husband live in Washington State. They have two grown children and six grandchildren. Wanda and Richard often travel the country, visiting their many Amish friends and gathering further information about the Amish way of life. In her spare time, Wanda enjoys photography, ventriloquism, gardening, reading, stamping, and having fun with her family. Visit Wanda's website at www.wandabrunstetter.com and to learn more about her children's books, visit www.amishfictionforkids.com.